JACK RIVERS AND ME

PAUL JOHN RADLEY

Jack Rivers and Me

TICKNOR & FIELDS · NEW YORK

1986

First American edition, 1986

Library of Congress Cataloging in Publication Data

Radley, Paul, 1962–
Jack Rivers and me.

I. Title.
PR9619.3.R22J3   1986   823   85-20681
ISBN 0-89919-429-X
ISBN 0-89919-433-8 (pbk.)

Printed in the United States of America

v 10 9 8 7 6 5 4 3 2 1

Jacket photograph by Allen Kurzweil

For

KENNY BETTS

*of Findlay, Ohio, a GI who came Down Under
with thousands of others when we needed them most*

A fair and slight and childish form,
With big brown dreamy eyes —
God help him! for a life of storm
And strife before him lies:
A wanderer and a gipsy wild,
I've learnt the world and know,
For I was such another child —
  Ah, many years ago!

Henry Lawson, "To Jim"

Since Jack Rivers is the only character in this book who ever had a chance of surviving, I want to assure those people who think (or imagine) they knew him that, yes, he is still around in many guises under many names, as busy as a drop of magnified water . . . alive and well and living in a transmuted bliss. But then, Jack was always so implantable.

JACK RIVERS AND ME

1

THE DISTURBED SILENCE of night was shedding its trust in darkness as its muted shafts of sound became one mobile daytime song: milkmen, paper boys, miners, cement workers, bike riders, motorists, shopkeepers, and early old amblers who could not sleep, all in their rising turns gave awakening power to the riddled morning.

It was nine-thirty before these mixed heralds of the day rested from their discrete and discordant rituals. After this sunrise ceremony of coming alive came the necessary rites of tethered living . . . day after day after week after month after year. World without end. Without question?

"Not on your bloody life, mate!"

The treadmill of simply surviving. There is no escape. Mountains are free. Oceans are unfettered, rivers escape, but men are held by their madness to possess. They bloodywell are!

"No. An individual is an utter world: his life a history."

So he is imprisoned within himself.

But this is a fireside argument: we're not talking about

the winters of living, we're talking about Eden Down Under. All that literal gouache . . .

"?"

. . . all right . . . all that indigestible goulash is not material. It's September. Spring is caterpillaring. There is a warm lip to the sunlight and the world is above horizons. Mount Kaiser is turbanned in mere quillings of cloud and the waters of Lake MacDonald reflect an azure-white gauze of sky. God's in *this* heaven even if all is not well with the rest of the world.

It is hard to believe that beneath the surface of this life-scape a crazy catharine wheel called day-before-school-starts is beginning to spin in half the homes of Boomeroo, a token town in the crease of the Lillipilli Valley, a long-settled unsleeping place in New South Wales, Australia.

"I don't wanna new pair of school pants, Mum . . . I like me old ones, patches an'll!"

"Mother, I need a new tunic; this's so faded: it's *puce*, not purple."

"Now, Jimmy, your school shoes go to Trevor, his goes to Brian, and I'm going to stain Marian's brown ones black for you . . ."

"Bum to that! I'll go barefoot first."

"Ted! Did you hear that?"

"Look, mate, if I hear another bloody word outa you you'll go to a new school altogether . . . *reform.*"

Ah, Boomeroo, where were you when my world was young and I was innocent as only the disinterested can be, and selfish as only the innocent are?

Ask a stupid question, get a stupid answer.

2

CONNIE DELARUE lay in bed trying to sort out the things she wanted to say to her young brother, Peanut, before his first day at school tomorrow.

"Deeeelaaaaroooo? What kinda name is that?" Duck Allsop said. "I thought yous was supposed to be Yanks, not Wogs."

Connie booted him in the shins and Duck chased her till he had her cornered in the telephone wing of the post office. As he was about to take his revenge one of Connie's side-kicks, Big Myrtle Worthington, hove out of the mail office and hauled into Duck with her ravaging school bag — a lingering punishment that made death seem like a super-market special on Saturday morning.

"Myrtle's big an' fat an' ugly with warts and a mighty stinky breath, but she sure is dependable!" Big Myrtle was as large and reliable as Connie's description.

Peanut was still in bed giving the usual good-morning bullshit to Jack Rivers. "Gee whizz, Jackie, I slept like a tin soldier. Did you sleep well, Jack?"

"Hell, I slept like forty hungry cats," Connie grumbled, cranking herself up on one elbow. She sounded as uncompromising as at least thirty hungry cats. "Thought you said Jack Rivers knew everything."

"Most things, I said," Peanut said awarely. He had a chirpy voice except when he was really sad and then he had the unhappiest voice this side of Mother Goose Without Tears.

"So what's he want to go to school for?"

"To be with me, Connie."

"What a lot of baby crap," Connie said, collapsing back into the soft foam of her big hospital bolster — a hand-me-down from her maternal grandmother.

"You confiscated it," Mum said.

"Well," Connie said, "what kind of Grandma gets married three times, then runs off to New Guinea leaving her two lovely grandchildren in their parents' clutches?"

"Jack Rivers, too," Peanut said. "He's in your clutches too, isn't he, Mum?"

"Johnnie, too," Mum said. She sometimes called Jack by this lovable name.

From the enormous hot embrace of the bolster — from which their grandmother used to exhort her first and second husbands' attention — Connie said, "I'll give you my best pair of wings and teach you to fly if you'll make Jack stay home." She hated condescending to bribery. Dad always said to have the guts to say what was on your mind and to hell with what was in the wind.

"I can't make him stay home," Peanut said with a particular chirp that could have driven a floorboard up the wall.

"Skip it!" Connie said and whopped out of bed. This was strange behaviour for someone who usually dragged herself out of bed like Big Fat Nellie all dressed up on the way to Kincomba, gauging the railway station steps as if they were Mount Kosciusko.

Both Peanut and Jack Rivers took this to mean it was going to be some strange kind of day. Soon after breakfast they knew it wasn't going to be hilarious. Connie sauntered after them like a rent-a-Vesuvius, passing casual fire in whews and phews.

"Fancy Gentleman Jack going to school tomorrow! He don't know so much after all."

"You're awful, Connie," Peanut said.

"I should care! Kid Rivers is a phoney an' means nothing to me. He doesn't buy my pyjamas. In fact . . . I hardly know him."

"But you once said . . ."

"What I once said and what I'm saying now," Connie shouted, "is my business and your misfortune. And tell me, what does your fribbly friend do for a crust, Peanut? If anything."

"Jack Rivers gets by."

Commandeering a phrase of their father's, Connie said, "And by whose goddamn standards does he get by? Jack Rivers is a bum kid! They're writing it on the fences."

"Sticks and bricks won't give me kicks," Peanut said, defiant for his Jack. "Jack doesn't give a bean for who's writing what on the fences. Jack wouldn't even look at that stuff."

"Because he can't read," Connie said. "Well, you tell him, my little chickenshit friend, that I'm writing it on the wall and I hope for his stupid sake he knows the difference. And quit walking round in *front* of me."

"But you're following us, Connie."

"Shut up, you dirty little sonofabitch!" She let them alone for an hour after that, until their mother went along to the store.

The Boys, dreading the bedevilled Connie, begged to be taken, but Nance Delarue did not decipher the urgency in her son's chirruping.

"Please, darling, stop harping," she said. "Stay home and behave and I'll get that leather school bag you liked and want so much." She hurried out, and they watched her skedaddle up Cambridge Street and cross the Main Road intersection the other side of the Death Seat . . .

"The *what?*"

The Death Seat. Can't we talk about it later?

"Is it a place where there's a lot of gory accidents?"

Oh, come off it.

"Wait-a-mo. I got it! It's like a public place . . . a *pissoir* . . . with seats. A shittoir? And all the local bards write . . ."

An accumulation of advice.

"Yeah! Like: *No use to kangaroo this seat; the crabs here jump fifteen feet.*"

No.

"Jesus slipt here?"

Some other time.

"Nobody wants to talk about the sulphur from the Cement Works either."

When Connie called them again the Two Boys were downstairs, very, very busy counting and contemplating carpet flowers behind the lounge suite in the living room. At Sunday School they had been told what happened to Christians when they went into the arena on a wild Saturday night in Rome. Maybe she'd get tired of calling.

The Fuller-Brush-Man she would! She came looking for them, walking painfully slow down the stairs like Fate dragging its feet and threatening a salvation smaller than life.

"Don't try to escape me. Big Sister is bigger than both of you. And I'm not some crummy serial on the wireless."

Their hiding places in the apartment were few, and a quick discounting of sulking places left only the refrigerator corner — a summer retreat — and where they were.

"Yah! Got you. I'm flesh and bloody here now even if you didn't answer when I called you." Her tremendous ink-blue eyes stabbed them, and her voice blasted their coordinate courage.

The silence was almost translucent. The Boys cringed and their lips moved in farouche shapes.

Connie squeezed behind the lounge and sat cross-legged in front of them, imprisoning them, wilfully sombre, her face a Goya nightmare. "Things are blue in Boomeroo, kids . . . and that's more than wrong in Binalong." The innominate gristle in her words chilled them.

These Two knew this was even more dreadful than when the chooks were crook in Muswellbrook on the Connie-scale of disaster. Peanut's eyes were frantically auditing a love he was sure existed beneath that mind-bending, sibling grimace: it was a wisp of bravery on his part.

"So what's Gentleman Jack got to say?"

A senseless knotted word.

"Don't think you can whinge-an'-win with me," Connie said. "Answer me properly or I'll spiflicate the pair of you."

Peanut's shoulders bucked, his head jumped and his eyes winced, shocking his tongue.

"If you're gonna take a fit like Fanny Kerr I'll stick a peg in your mouth so's you won't bite your tongue off."

"I don't take fits," Peanut said.

"He's gotta go, Peanut," she said.

"No, Connie, no!" So he had known what it was all about.

"The kids at school are waiting to *murder* him. They'll break ya heart, Peanut."

"He don't want to go away!"

"He *is* going," Connie said. "Even if I have to take him by the scruff of the neck and drag him out of this house."

Desperation explored a lot of heart territory and the whole dominion of his mind. "Don't take Jack away, Connie. We'll be so good. We'll wipe up the dishes every night because you hate that."

"Mum would only say you're too little."

"Well, I'll give you our best bird nest. And tell Mum we're big enough to run messages."

"But you're not big enough to go to the store."

"Connie? We could use your toothbrush so Mum'll think you've cleaned your teeth. And next Christmas we'll only ask for one pillowslip for toys instead of two . . . and . . . Jackie will give you that Christmas card he got *From Santa*. 'Member?"

Oh, my God, that Christmas card was worth its weight in hummingbirds. His baby bargaining was getting through her defence. Connie was too much the offensive fighter. This infighting began to rip her.

"It's for his own good, Peanut. I'll pack a little bag and put him on the Express this evening."

"Why?" There had to be a limit to the agony of a childhood ache.

"You know why. Jack will be OK. He's a rover. You always said he could look after himself. So . . . the time has come."

"But Jack likes it here."

"He's been here too long," Connie said. "You don't want him to wear his welcome out?"

"That's for Mum to say," Peanut said, almost as corruptly as Connie quoted Dad.

"Look, kid, I'm older and bigger than you . . ."

"I don't want to hear that again."

". . . and I know."

"Well, don't tell me!"

Connie gripped him by the shoulders. He flinched and shut his eyes. "You will listen." His sister's voice was volcanic and her words the lava of destruction. "Even some of the kids in the Big School are waiting to rib the rotten Almighty out of Jack Rivers. And Duck Allsop is gonna sool his dirty big black retriever onto him. I can look after you at school, but not the both of you."

"Jack will look after all of us."

"Goddamn you, don't give me that crap! Can't you see what they'll do to you if you stick up for him . . . you . . . drongo."

"You're never s'posed to call me a drongo. Mum said not to!" Peanut feebled out and his world sagged in an atlas of defeated thoughts.

Australia dragged a frozen-arsed Tasmania out of the Antarctic. India was a stalactite proportion. Africa had Nigerian dropsy and South America was pregnant rather than breasty. His whole mentality was as pooped as a Dali painting.

Little Brother peeked from the ashes of hope just to make sure the world *was* coming to an end and gave Big Sister a last desperate, big-sick-fat-eye look that always worked on Mum.

"Buy yourself a battery, buster," Connie said. "Your lights just went out."

Peanut was nothing if not inventive in retreat: he smiled his chubbiest, sucked his teeth with a kisslike movement, then pursed his mouth in a sipping sound. Charlie Chaplin was never better.

"Skip the photo finish," Connie said. "Laurel and Hardy aren't around, Dad's loaned his movie camera to Mr. Canwell, and Mum's Brownie's on the blink."

The world re-formed miraculously: after all even Peanut knew it wasn't flat.

"Well, can Jack stay here till morning and then go to the

Express by himself. If it's . . . *Absolooly Imperative*. I'd like to spend the last day before school with him. He can tell me things that you couldn't."

"Hah . . . a likely story," Connie said.

Peanut's fingers fiddled up and down the leaf-ladder bordering the carpet; his silence was defiant, and Connie knew just how stubborn he could be.

"And you promise he'll go in the morning?"

Peanut nodded; he couldn't be bothered with the legalities and was only glad that Jack hadn't been involved verbally in the showdown. In such a cantankerous mood Connie could smash steel to smithereens. If Jack Rivers opened his mouth now . . . *wouf* . . . she would rip him from Frisco to St. Jo, as Dad said. As she had many other constructed ventures. It took a lot of will power for Jack to remain mum, for he was intelligent and intransigent — and did not have a sponge heart.

"Spit-ya-death-and-cut-ya-throat." Connie was relentless: in a sense Kid Rivers was escaping her real wrath. She lifted her brother's chin while he took the oath.

"I promise." Peanut spat drily and executed the throat-and-finger drill which was more binding than Armistice. An avalanche of renewed love for his quiet buddy swept him and he shivered.

"I'll settle for that." Connie snatched her hand away and his face dropped. "Some day you'll understand and be happy for what I did."

Defeated, Peanut was not that same baby. *"No, I won't,"* he said. "I'll never-never-never be glad about it." And that was anathematically that. Never-never-never was about as long as his hate could revolt and further than his imagination could recoil: Darwin and God notwithstanding.

The inquisition over, Connie strolled through the kitchen, looked into the laundromat where her father was bulling a few hefty housewives, went outside and kicked every gibber in the back yard, then locked herself in the lavatory and cried. The guilts had her. Voluminous tears welled through her clenched eyes and seeped into her gaping mouth. She hooked her bottom lip under her top teeth but irretainable anger kept busting her open. She punched her knees and ground her inadequate teeth, trying to hate herself enough to punish herself. Finally she gave up and let the passion and the pent-upness rack itself out.

Peanut and Jack Rivers remained in their vanquished kingdom, unable to believe that only this very morning everything had been so sunny in their wandering wonderful world. Just yesterday they had been mad with the power of being loved and wanted, riding chariots of joy through the rooms.

"Look out, Mum! Here come the car racers! Jack and me are the world champs."

"Wouldn't I know my Boys would be world champions," Mum said, flicking an Irish linen tea-towel at them.

"How come all the fuckin' tea-towels in the world come from Ireland?"

"Because the Irish never wash up, wipe up or wipe their arses, grub; so what they gonna do with all that linen?"

Peanut and Jack Rivers wondered what had happened to yesterday but didn't give a fig where tomorrow was coming from. In Connie-punctured memories they sought past happinesses.

"I'll never forget you either, Jack. You'll always be My Jack. You will remember me wherever you roam, won't you? Don't cry. It's too late. We spat-our-death-and-cut-our-throat and promised. And you die if you break a promise."

And who in their pie-eating mind would want to die

before they were ten, when they'd be old enough for a two-wheeler bike? Besides, dying before you were old enough to be a high school boy would be . . . a *Real Perdicament.*

After their mother returned from shopping, Connie foraged for a piece of chalk and went down to the concrete culvert adjacent to the Highway Bridge where the kids wrote their protests against life and their attitude toward adultimatums. There was very little nitty-gritty graffiti in evidence, although someone had once painted a gigantic black FUCK there which now framed the whole protesting wall. Most of it was day-to-day griping or overnight hate, with some imaginative loving:

PARENTS ARE POOP

HATA CUCUMBA ADAY

DUCK PLAYS WITH HIS D B B R

HOW DO YOU SPELL POOFTA

ASK MR. ROWLANDSON

MISS CRUIKSHANK LOVES SWIFTIE MADISON

ME TOO   ME TOO   I DO TOO

SWIFTIE LOVES SWIFTIE THE MOST

GUTSA IS A BLUDGER

MY OLD MAN IS A GRUB

MRS. HAWK SHOWED ME HER THING

MY OLD MAN IS A GRUB TOO

The large and small complaints were innumerable but any quick addition or fast discounting between fact and fancy soon revealed that, above and beyond the intense dislike of Kincomba and Cucumbers, Swiftie Madison was

the town's best-loved honey and Duck Allsop the least
loved if not the most reviled . . . with Gutsa Mevinney and
Mr. Rowlandson in hot pursuit in the hate stakes.

Connie chose a spot between:

SCHOOLS ARE FOR FOOLS

GOD HATES CUCUMBERS

THEY MAKE HIM BURP

and . . .

I WISH CRUIKSHANK WAS MY MUM

NOBODY CARES ABOUT ME

ME EITHER

. . . where, in a soft glissading of tears she scrawled effec-
tively and with fervent deliberation:

CONNIE DELARUE IS A BITCH

SHE SURE IS

After that she hung around the railway station dating up
passengers on the few slow-passing trains and scratching
arrival and departure times from the Express timetable.
She also spent half an hour being mean to busy ants, lazy
snails, bewildered butterflies and insignificant insects no
matter how beautiful or defenceless they were.

She meandered home, throwing stones at dogs and kick-
ing friendly cats, knowing she was late for lunch and looking forward to the bawling-out she would get from her
father and the plausible complaints she might or might not
get from her mother . . . depending how involved Nance
was with Peanut and Jack Rivers, with cleaning, sewing,

cooking or listening to crummy wireless serials such as that bloody Big Sister (what a dumb-dumb!) or Those Feveral Girls.

Those fuckin' Feveral Girls? I know what they're up to. I know what that means. Big Myrtle's done it with her uncle, an' told me about it.

"Nobody cares about me, either. Poor Peanut . . . he don't even know he's a boy, and you gotta be a boy to get anywhere. As for Jack Rivers . . . I'd sell him to Mr. Rowlandson. How *do* you spell poofter, I wonder?"

3

NANCE DELARUE is sitting on the Death Seat, that big bench at the corner of Main Road and Cambridge Street, which more people have used than have abused the walls of the Kincomba Domain public toilets. Monte Howard is slumped at the other end: he missed the school train again this morning and won't get another to take him to Kincomba High for two hours. He's never been the same boy since his pigeon, Corker, died; but if there is an answer to his torment he knows he'll find it here.

These two, confined in vices of silence and sorrow, will find their hearts eased and their pain soothed. That's what the Death Seat's for. To relieve grief and give them the comfort of all the time in the world, which it has and they have not.

Nance Delarue is not sure that she can go on without Jack Rivers, the quiet fellow who curled into the most hospitable spot in her heart, where only Peanut had ever been before. Admit it, Nance, Connie was never in that safest of all places.

To have lost Jack on this same day as she had figuratively been forsaken by the schoolboy, Peanut, was a shock she had not anticipated. A catastrophe she had never thought likely. Jack Rivers so all of a sudden . . . gone. He might as well be dead. No! She mustn't think that, for when Peanut was grown and married with children of his own Johnnie would still be completely hers; in her heart wherever he might be.

She often wondered if the male canopy in this small boisterous town was the real reason her American husband, Tony, was as happy as he claimed to be in Australia. The women leaning on the fences and the men leaning on the pub bar: what futures did they offer one another? And only their similar but disconnected pasts to offer their children. Mrs. Allsop was right when she referred to some people as sophs.

Mrs. Allsop was not only wont to say but said-away: "Don't take any notice of Tottie Carruthers, Nellie; she's a bit of a soph, you know."

Or, if it suited her perverse reasoning: "Ignore her, Tottie; Nellie Whitehead's a real soph."

In Allsopiana, a soph was an undeniable and undefendable second-class peasant. It was an anagram made on posh and had nothing to do with sophistication. In the early days it was plainly aimed at arriving pommies and clearly meant: Starboard Out, Port Home. And you couldn't get any second-classer than that.

In the scaffolding of their lives, these women were happy. Not Nance. All she had ever wanted to be was a schoolteacher — one who sought truths. She envied Miss Cruikshank.

Kate Cruikshank had reported to her schoolchildren every school day for over forty years. And each and every day a trellis of bright young eyes and a circuit of anxious little ears had sought her intelligence with an attention and need an unfed computer would envy: to become a distorted but truly loved legend in the misty maze of local recall.

Nance's husband, Tony Delarue, was certainly doing a good job of serving his Aussie apprenticeship of that greatest of all Down Under trades: pub-grubbing.

"A beer in the hand is worth more than a paddock of barley in the bush."

Pub-grubbers revelled in the sovereignty of the Australian Pub, the most powerful trade union in this deceasing world. Now the new beer gardens in New South Wales were giving those women who had never been able to lick their men a chance to join them. The housewives went to sit and sip and shell peas for tea, and slander the absentees. Pub-scrubbing.

Nance would remain on the Death Seat until she unwound and discovered a few home truths about herself. Alone like this, she found the emotional landscape eventually cleared. It took time: truth was not easily compartmentalized. For all that she tried to be an individual, Mrs. Delarue was not the kind of person who could grow a Moreton Bay fig tree in her back yard and to hell with her neighbours. The ethical beauty of the Death Seat *was* being there with oneself no matter who else was sharing the big bench. Even in this hick town most people came here to wash their minds in preference to going to church to listen to the repeated idioms of their professed religions.

"Except the Catholics. The tykes do go to church regularly, you gotta say that for them."

"Because they're mostly Irish an' the Shamrocks don't wash much any other way," Mrs. Allsop said. She was of Scottish descent.

How the Scotch have descended!

Sitting on the Death Seat was to feel time and peace furl

about you as soundlessly as dew. No tears now, Nance. No tears. If your future is no more cruel to you than your past you'll laugh again. To have experienced the Death Seat is enough to give you the will to search for its criteria in other moments; with insight you will find what you are looking for in yourself, and sometimes in others.

There is no link missing between men. Though some are weak and some are loose, all the links are there, waiting for the drawing together, not the herding. And sooner or later every single person in his most profound or most wilful moment knows he belongs to all men.

The trees in Cambridge Street came from many lands and, with the exception of the pencil pine in front of the billiard room and those camphor laurels protecting the school playground, their leafy weeping through May and June distracted traffic. In September and October their greening joy brought magic contrast to the droves of eucalyptus sweeping over and along the hillsides and hemming the highways like dusty grey-olive tidal waves.

Nance Delarue was always proud that the tree in front of their shop, the Cambridge Laundrette, was first to bud. Her tree, she thought; but she knew that Peanut and Jack Rivers called it their tree. The sun illuminating the tiny leaves in the early spring congratulated her waking moment and she would lie there, hardly breathing lest she disturb Tony into withdrawing his arm from across her breasts. Thinking how the sun was already higher over Boolawoy Beach than it was over Boomeroo . . .

"Ever noticed from the hills how the Boolawoy sand dunes look like a lot of bodies . . . a sort of orgy of naked women?"

"That was just all those Sydney schoolteachers on holidays what you saw."

. . . and how, before Boolawoy it had risen over Norfolk

Island . . . and before that had awakened some Fijian from his grass-matted bure, some Samoan from his wall-less fale. Previous to that, a descendant of Fletcher Christian's on Pitcairn . . . and earlier still a lonely herder in the Andes. Some South African, black, brindle or white (apartheidized or otherwise) after soaking the Seychelles with light. And before it had warmed the waters of the Indian Ocean it must have disturbed . . .

A disgruntled housewife in Perth?

That would stump Nance. She knew very well that the woman in Perth was still fast asleep waiting for this very same leaf-lighting sun to ride over Boomeroo, cross the Great Dividing Range, search the outback, wake the Alice, finger Ayres Rock, prescribe dawn for the Nullabor Plain . . . and then . . . chuck sunlight farther west to where Fremantle beached the Indian Ocean. The same sun!

Then she would fondle Tony's penis for a soft moment before she threw herself out of bed, bouncing his arm away from her body. She had to be quick at this because once his mind was aroused and his prick hard Tony was ever ready for . . .

"Beddies and baddies, and you kiss Daddy's?" . . . prolonged play.

"Shit, Nance," Tony said, "you're getting like a cup of hot coffee . . . only good for ten goddamn minutes."

Sitting on the Death Seat after enrolling Peanut in school, Nance thought how that same tree protected her from the hotter summer sun, and how the bigger leaves were so shady she had trouble adjusting her physical alarm. She had to wake up before seven-thirty because that was her husband's awakening time. It was uncanny, his sexual alarm. If he was first awake there was no way out of it. He would have her gentled and horny and wanting him more than breakfast before she realized she was no longer asleep. One of these mornings Connie was going to wake up early, barge in and catch them at it. Yet, at night, even when she tried hard, it never came to the same crystallizing conclusion.

The Death Seat was gentling her now.

"Of course, I'd like to be more than just an accomplice in love," Nance once said to her visiting mother. "But I guess just being a *mother* is supposed to be more enlarging — and I use the word sardonically — than painlessly becoming a father."

"You'd have trouble stringing those beads in mixed company in this town," her expatriate mother said.

"Women ought to be thankful they've got men to do what's necessary to fulfill their lives," Tony said, coming home beautifully boozy.

"Spoken like a man," his mother-in-law said, "with a race guide in one hand and a beer in the other."

"Go home to Sparta," Tony said.

"Never do anything for a man that you expect credit or thanks for," her mother said to Nance.

"Does a woman who marries three times give thanks for things she doesn't get, expect or get credit for?"

"A woman who marries more than once doesn't leave a churned-up wake like the *Queen Mary* behind her," the *grand* mother said.

"You could douche yourself with that," Nance said.

"For Godsake!" Tony said. "I never heard so much crap galore in my life before."

Neither of them answered him, but both turned and gave him a common look that described him rather than welcomed his comment. He grinned and opened the palms of his hands apologetically.

Nance wondered if she loved Tony less the more Aussie he became. Yes, she did love him less. God, how she had loved him for his American difference when they'd first married. Or did she love him less because Peanut and Jack had stolen some of her love away from him? Or because Connie had taken so much of his love away from her?

What was it Mrs. Allsop said about people who lived in the pub. "People who live in glass houses ain't game to go home."

Nance closed her eyes and relaxed to give the Death Seat a full chance to absorb her; her mind had become too busy. A sun-rinsed pale blue sky embraced the world of the valley around her. She sensed Monte Howard leave in the rustle of a movement. Then she was authoritatively alone with Whoever was Standing In for God that morning.

"OK. So the Death Seat's big medicine. We've gathered that."

You're a spindrift lot of sons-of-bitches . . .

"Bastards to you. But don't worry about us, mate. We all got wives and kids we can belt shit outa when we go home unhappy from work or the pub or the two-up . . ."

Or the races or the dogs or the billiard room or the fire station corner?

4

JACK RIVERS and me are just lying in bed this morning wondering . . . that's all, just wondering. Mum says we'll never set the world on fire but we'll never burn a school-house down either. We wonder about that. Like we wonder where we came from; and often wish we had been here before Connie, rat-damn it!

Do you ever think back real hard, as far back as you can? We do . . . all the time. And we wonder about a lot of other things. Why the sky is not green and the creek not a pretty red. Why dogs bark but don't talk. That kind of stuff. Wouldn't it be nice if puppies could talk back at you when you spoke to them? Why Mum and Dad make funny noises in bed sometimes.

One thing we don't have to wonder about is why we love each other, Jack and me. We just do and that's all there is to that on a fine day in Manchester . . . wherever that is! The world could fall apart at the seams and we'd hardly notice. In fact that's exactly what Dad says about us when he comes home looped from the pub looking for an

argument (and gets one) when Mum tells him what That
Good Lady thinks of the mob holding up the bar in the
Sulphide Hotel when it's raining in Melbourne . . . wherever
that may be. Sometimes we do wish that people would tell
us where all these places are in the rest of the world.

"You're getting like Those Two Boys, Nance," Dad said.
"The world could fall apart at the seams and You Three
wouldn't notice so long as the table's set at six and cleared
by seven. Goddamn it, I'll have my supper at breakfast
time in Woop Woop if I feel like it. And if I don't feel like
it you can warm it up and send it to the starving bloody
masses in Asia as far as I'm concerned."

When Dad says supper he means teatime because he's a
Yank; but one thing I do know . . . *nobody* knows where
Woop Woop is. If we peek under the bedside table we can
see Connie asleep. She is ten, counting up to eleven faster
than she's growing fingers . . . and sleeps by herself.

"I'm pretty grown up now," Connie said to Mum and
Dad. "When are You Guys gonna get me a room of my
own? I'm sleeping with babies yet!"

"Very soon, dear," Mum said. "When you learn to speak
good English."

"That a crack at me?" Dad said.

"Be that as it may," Mum said sweetly.

"Parents!" Connie said not at all sweetly.

If you ever came to our house and it was dark or if you
were blind, you'd still know my Mum by the sound of
sugar in her voice . . . mostly. If you could hear sugar.
That's if you weren't deaf.

"That Peanut!" Connie said. "He beats about the bush
like as if he'd lost a piece of licorice in the black stump."

What's the good of telling you Connie talks loudly when
most of the time she yells or roars. Better if I just tell you
if she . . . ever . . . whispers.

"Your brother is still searching for words, Connie, and is

simply using expressions he hears from other people . . . whether he really understands them or not. Give him time." Mum winked at me.

"Talkin' about time . . . it's time to talk about when and if I'll ever get me own room," Connie said.

"Them's fightin' words," Dad said, jostling Connie round the room and shaping up to her. "Come on, ya brat; put ya dooks up!"

Connie's pretty good with the flying fists, I must admit from experience, but I'm afraid Dad's the poor man's Les Darcy. When my sister has a gripe she calls us You Guys, and bundles Mum and Dad and Jack and me all in the same packet of peanuts; but we don't mind because we like being bundled with Dad. She sure is a sleepyhead, but. Just look at her this morning: dead as a doorstep. Still if you call out to her in the night when you've got the willies, she does come. Grumbly-like, but she comes.

"All right, Boys, back to sleep. The blue divils have gone. You must've been havin' a nightmare. There's no one here 'cept us . . . *ghosts*." Connie's a bit of a lark at times but she's good to have around in the dark. "I'm only kidding! I'd knock pockets offa any ghost came within undressin' distance of this bedroom. I'd rip his sheet to hankies!"

"You are brave, Connie."

"Compared to You Two, Humpty Dumpty was brave."

"Oh . . . Jack's brave enough when it's necessary."

"Like Henny-penny. I'd stack him up against Chicken Little if I was on the Selection Committee . . . and have all me money on the chook."

Connie hardly ever wakes up before eight o'clock, when she smells the toast. And if she smells it burning, watch out walls. She gets kicky and crabby.

"Oh, my God! Burnt toast again? That Woman in the

kitchen (Mum) sure is a lousy short-order cook. I gotta ask Dad again why he ever married her in the first and last place."

Jack and me, we love burnt toast. And know what? Mum sometimes specially burns it for us (I think) though it does sometimes strike me and Jack that Mum might say she burnt it for us when she did it accidentally. But that would be shoofty, wouldn't it? And Mum's more sugary than shoofty, take my word for it. Or take *Jack's* word for it. So you see, it is a bit of a *perdicament* when Connie makes this rip-snortin' fuss over a bit of black toast. If you were Mum what would you do in such a perdicament?

On the other foot I sometimes figure Mum is getting to the stage where she doesn't care how much Connie rants on.

"That Young Lady is a whole crusade of affectations, and I'm fast becoming immune to her Jerusalems," Mum said. Whatever that means.

Maybe Jack and me are not crusaders but we are a lot of other things . . .

"Dumb dills to begin with," Connie said.

"I heard that!" Mum said.

Mum says, "I heard that!" quite a fair bit. Oh, I forgot to tell you that my name is James Oxford Delarue, if you want to put it in the papers, but everybody calls me Peanut. Don't ask me why. I don't know why, that's why. Dad started it then forgot about it and now he's likely to call me anything but Peanut . . . like Fella, Son, Junior (I hate that) or Bub, and (heavens) sometimes even Goober. And just lately the Jimbarella Kid.

"Don't ask me why," Mum said. "I haven't the vaguest idea where Jimbarella is; but if your father's heard of it I bet it's a good pub town."

"Junior!" Connie said. "I wouldn't call the little rat Junior in my Devil-meanest mood."

(Let's not even think about Connie at her Devil meanest.)

Sometimes Dad just calls me Jim. And listen to this: if he's in his Holy-Cincinnati-it's-the-4th-of-July mood he might even call Jack, Johnnie. Well . . . he has . . . once!

When Mum tucks us into bed and says: Good night Peanut, good night Jack, she sounds nicer than the bell on the ice cream cart, and little bits of us shiver like jelly.

"Why does Dad call the ice cream man a good-rumour man? Is he better'n Mrs. Allsop, Mum?"

"It's good-humour man! Maybe because he puts You Boys in a good mood."

"Tell me what kind of baby I was again."

"You were a fubsy-bubsy baby. And I'm sure Jack was, too."

Sometimes Mum will sit with us and tell us about when her mother, Laura Eva Oxford, was a little girl. Laura Eva Oxford sure seems to have had a long life because she's our Granny and it's still going on.

"Laura Eva Oxford, indeed," Connie said. "One of these days I'm gonna pin that woman down and get the true story of her endless life out of her."

"If you don't want to listen you can turn over and go to sleep," Mum said.

"It's worse than a wireless serial," Connie said.

"Well, that's the end of tonight's episode in any case, Boys," Mum said.

"What a way to end a day!" Connie said. "Up to your ears in Laura Eva Whatever-her-name-is-now-in-Papua."

Connie thinks she is the Big Pig in the family, but Dad is really because he decides what we're going to listen to on the wireless when we're all sitting around it at night . . . and that seems to be the Big Pig's job in any family round here.

Dad calls Mum, Nance, and Mum calls Dad either

Antony or Tony, or even Waldo. *Waldo?* Don't ask me. I'm supposed to brush my teeth and say my prayers every night. Usually I brush my teeth and Jack says the prayers. I'll tell you when I *do* say my prayers, but. That's the nights when I remember that Dad is a Waldo: then I whip onto my knees real fast and say my prayers and thank God that I'm not a Waldo.

Connie sometimes calls Dad, Tony, and Mum, Nance . . . when she's mad with them and can't say anything worse than what she's allowed to say aloud. And if she says Nancy-pants she makes it sound worse still. Don't ask me how. Connie can do things like that. And when she wants to get round Dad she can even make Waldo sound cute. If you think that's easy, well you try it some time. Dad thinks it's funny. But that hog-wog don't wash with Mum because Mum is supposed to be down-to-earth.

When Jack and me are sick-and-tired of Connie's goings-on and wish we were able to stand up to her (when we feel like ripping her apart for a change) we call her That One . . . if she's not around to hear us. You could say that Connie makes life pretty tenterhooky.

Connie and Dad are buddies, and Jack and me and Mum are mates. Sometimes Connie and Dad get cranky with each other and give each other real ding-dong punches. My sister is a dirty all-in fighter and one day she cracked hell out of Saul Hamilton (even though she secretly loves him) because he said she liked Hedley Detley, who has a sister called Sedley Detley . . . and . . . oh forget it. Jack and me and Mum, we never fight: we love each other so much just as if we lived together close as close as you could get in a little house far away from the rest of the world . . . and let it fall apart at the seams if it wants to.

"Come away with me, Boys," Mum said. "Let the rest of the world go bye-bye!"

"Yuk," Connie said. "You Three make me wanta chuck when you go on like as if cuddles was money."

"You're too commercial, Con," Mum said. "Let your hair down and join in the fun."

"Call that fun?" Connie said. "I see flies in spiderwebs havin' more fun than that. Duck Allsop has better fun with his dirty big black retriever, and he's a stupid bodgie."

"What's a bodgie, Connie?"

"A drongo who's younger than a grub but thinks he's old enough to have a widgie."

"What's a widgie?"

"A bodgie's girl, of course. Can't you even add one and one?"

"Yes. And you know I could add up to ten before I was two . . . Mum said!"

"You the grubs' Einstein?"

Once The Three Rovers (Mum calls us that) built a cubby of cushions in the living room, and we had buckets of fun. My, we laughed.

"I feel so Alicey in here we might as well have a tea party," Mum said. "Peanut, you can be the Mad Hatter and Jack can be the White Rabbit." Truly. Mum said that. Jack could be the White Rabbit.

We had real tea, too; not just this-must-be-tea and I-must-be-mother stuff. We used Connie's tea set, but that's a bomb secret.

"We'll all go up in smoke if Connie finds out," Mum said, "even though she never uses it."

"I don't want all that Curly-Shirley junk," Connie once said, "but don't you give it to Those Boys, Nance. Next they'll want my old dolls!"

"The surviving wrecks," Mum said. "Those you haven't murdered or brutally buried alive."

"Even dolls die, Nance," Connie said. "But I will keep

what's left in case you and Waldo have another baby . . . but it better be a girl, that's all I've got to say about it. And I'm gonna call her Rhodelia."

"Thanks a lot but no thanks," Mum said. "And you'd have nothing . . . absolutely nothing to say about it."

"I wouldn't even call a rabbit Rhodelia," I said. Sometimes I do have my say. And I love it when Mum says Absolooly.

"I certainly don't want a rabbit to pass all my gear and know-how on to," Connie said.

"Pass it on to Johnnie and Peanut," Mum said.

"Not on your sweet-nothing life," Connie said. "They're imbos!"

"That's enough, Connie!" Mum said, because imbo is supposed to be a worse word than drongo. "You can wait and have your own . . . Rhodelia. I can hardly bring myself to say the name." Mum shivered her eyes at Jack and me.

"It's a cross between Rhoda and Bedelia," Connie whispered sneakily. "That's the names of those two girls I read about in the Sydney paper who murdered their ninety-year-old auntie and run off with her hidden money."

"I said that's enough, Connie. Funny is funny but that is not!"

"When I'm ninety," Connie said, "I won't care which way I go."

Mum knew it was no use telling Dad because he went on like that sometimes on Sunday when it was too late to get beer from the back door of the pub and there was only lolly-water left in the icebox.

Dad calls the refrigerator an icebox but Mum says iceboxes went out before I was born. "Besides we used to call them icechests."

"Icechest?" Dad said. "Sounds like a disease they die from in Alaska."

Sometimes Connie's more like a mum and Mum's more like a sister. Mum would make a good sister but I dread to think of Connie as my mother. It's enough to make my rocking horse shiver. If Connie was a mother you'd wonder what God made mothers for . . . and it wouldn't be a song your granny sings.

"Where the hell did you come from, Connie?" Dad said. "I swear you've been here before."

Mum's different. She's like a little girl grown up. I wish I could explain how we really feel about her. Like as if there wouldn't be any world or anything at all without her. When we first open our eyes in the morning and they are a bit cobwebby, and we try to remember where we are, and what we did before we went to bed . . . and things are fuzzled . . . we remember Mum. Then suddenly we are full of a sort of jumpy-joy. Like the breeze waking up the curtains. And you can see her smiling at you even though she's downstairs getting breakfast. If you think about your mum for a minute you'll know exactly what I mean. As long as your mum isn't a Connie.

"Just to smell Mum around the house is enough," Dad said.

"I'm not sure I like that," Mum said. Mum's a great I'm-not-surer.

"The only times she smells good to me is when she's wearing that Evening in Paris I gave her for Christmas," Connie said. "Not that I'd be found dead with a drop of it on me."

"We love whatever you smell like, Mummy, Jack Rivers and me."

"Dadadadadadadadadadadadah," Connie and Dad sang together.

I'm not so sure that Dad loves Jack Rivers. Mum says he does. She says Dad has to work so hard to keep us in clothes and ice cream and lollies and food and to keep the wolf from the door and a roof over our heads, and the Insurance Man happy, that he doesn't always have time to show us he loves us. So Jack and me think if he just kept us in clothes and ice cream and lollies and let the house keep the roof over our heads . . .

"To hell with the Insurance Man," Connie said. "Who's he when he's home in pyjamas, anyway?"

. . . my Jack Rivers could keep the wolf from the door. But last we heard there wasn't a wolf within cooee of this town. Between you and me and Jack and the gatepost I wouldn't want to be any wolf at our door if Connie answered it. He'd be lucky to get away with his belly-button covered. She'd have a fur kite and a new hunting cap before you could say Three Little Pigs. You should see the trap she's building just to catch Duck Allsop's dirty big black retriever. Well, it's this . . . enormous box kite, really. Once she gets that poor dog into that kite it's a goner. If it ever comes into our back yard that dirty big black retriever will wish his mother had been a cow . . .

"He won't need to bark at the moon where he's goin'," Connie said.

Connie's kite-happy. She also makes flying wings, and tries to fly.

"Tony! Speak to Connie," Mum said. "She's been flying again."

"Hullo, Connie," Dad said.

"It's not funny," Mum said. "Flying's not ladylike."

"Neither is Connie," Dad said. He can be a bit of a wag at times.

"I mean it's tomboyish and dangerous," Mum said.

"If it was good enough for Amy Johnson and Bert Hinkler . . ." Connie said.

"And the Wright boys," Dad said.

Mum flew off the handle then and said a wicked word. You might as well know; Mum's also a fly-off-the-handler.

Jack and me, we didn't say a word, but you know what? Flying is wonderful! Connie took Jack for a fly one day. That's a secret. I bet you think Jack and me are terrible for keeping a secret from Mum. You see, Connie is all right, sometimes. It's a fact, we have a hard time trying to hate her. At least she does talk to Jack: Dad never really talks to him . . . maybe asks about him. He did say good night to Jack once, but Jack always says good night to Dad because he's a perfect little gentleman. Mum says so.

"Gentleman Jack Rivers," Connie said. "You sneaky cobber from Awaba."

"He is my cobber but he's not from Awaba."

"You're not sure where he came from."

"I know about Awaba, but. Dad said that's where they put a keg of beer on a stump on Saturday night and it ain't Sunday till the men are all too pissed to go to church. See! And Jackie sure didn't come from a place like that."

"So where is Jack-God-Rivers from, pray?"

"Everywhere." You've got to be careful when Connie uses that word: pray. It sure means trouble the way Connie constructs it; you'd think it was a Meccano word . . . or like as if she met Jesus on a busy corner and was asking Him to stand aside without so much as a please or thank you.

"Don't dance round the maypole with me," Connie said. "Do you or don't you know where he's from?"

Connie tries to pin me down in lots of ways, but when I've got me paddy up I try to worm my way out of it. I am wormy and sneaky sometimes, but not shoofty. Between you and me and the cuckoo clock I haven't got the faintest idea where my mate was born.

"Jack comes from a place where there's plenty of real *big* things in life going on."

"Like the Royal Easter Show in Sydney," Connie said. "At least he wasn't born at Christmas like Jesus. The way you glox on I thought he mighta been Holy."

Isn't she a bobby-dazzler? She makes up words too, you'll notice.

"I'll be glad when she gets to Miss Cruikshank's class and gets taken down a peg or two," Mum said. "I wish she was more gentle like you and Jack. Johnnie's such a gentle boy."

I think Mum loves all gentle boys. When she was a girl she knew this gentle boy called Mitch Singleton. My, that boy must have been so gentle I don't know how on earth he ever survived.

"He didn't! The *war* got him," Connie said. Mum's right; she ain't . . . isn't a bit gentle.

I think Jack gets round Connie mainly because he's a change . . . no . . . I mean challenge. Once I was in bed sick. Well, I've been in bed sick more than once, but this time I was head-and-vomity sick, not just tummy sick. For two long weeks I was this yellow yukkie colour. I tell you, it was a time to keep away from mirrors. Well . . . you know what . . . you're not going to believe this after the way I've been chiacking about her . . . Connie took Jack Rivers for a walk. Sat with him on the Death Seat for a while, then went up to the post office for Dad and showed Jack the sacred place where Big Myrtle Worthington whaled the holy-livin'-daylights out of Duck Allsop. Walked him back along the creek where they paddled barefoot for longer than they should have. Took him *under* the railway bridge and waited for a coal train from Bora Bora to thunder over the top of them. *Then* raced across Highway Bridge while the coal train finished crossing the creek and made its big turn on the Wollondonga loop-line and waited there until it hissed underneath them and the warm furry smoke came up and fussed around their feet.

"You'll be giving Peanut ideas," Mum said.

"But, Mum," Connie said, "Jack Rivers *took me*. I had to be quick to keep up with him."

"You're getting too fast for your own tongue," Mum said. "Don't go too far, Young Lady." Mum's always telling someone they go too far . . . but they never leave.

"Jack Rivers wanted to catch the smoke," Connie persisted — I think that's something sisters do well. "I'm not that dumb."

"You'll catch something . . . and the smoke will be your backside burning," Mum said.

Jack loved that walk and told me that Connie was only defending herself and not dobbing him in . . . which you could understand in such a perdicament. So this is what we try to remember when Connie is nasty. "Think about the good times, Jack," I say when Connie's in war paint.

"You Boys. Come here and face the music," Connie's liable to say. And we know it isn't going to be "Cradle Song."

"Is Jack sick too, Mrs. Delarue?" the doctor said.

"Oh no, Doctor. Jack is never sick," Mum said.

"He looks peaked to me," Connie said.

After that the doctor and Mum . . . Had Words.

"It is a perdicament," the doctor said.

"Why can't he go to hospital, Nance?" Dad said. "They can do so much more for him there."

"Oh, Antony, don't you realize they won't take Jack into hospital with him," Mum said from a long way away.

"My God," Dad roared. "This is going too far! If the Jimbarella Kid (that's me) doesn't start getting better from today on he goes to Kincomba Hospital like Dr. Freeman suggested."

"Not unless it's absolooly imperative," Mum said and gritted her big front teeth.

"You want he should die, Nance?"

"And do you want to break his heart?"

"That does it!" Dad yelled. "Jack Rivers goes! To hell and high water out of this house. That is *it*, Nance. You understand . . . honey?"

"There's an aspect here . . . a psycholo . . ."

"I don't want to hear it, thank you, Doctor," Dad said . . . rudely too. You've never heard *rudies* till you've heard my Dad.

"If Jack Rivers leaves this house tonight," Mum said as quiet as a kitten but looking like a lion, and trembly and close too, "Peanut and I go with him."

Daddy stared down at me and I could see wet little stars in his eyes. Then he stomped downstairs like a Baddie.

I couldn't understand why Jack wouldn't be allowed in Cucumber Hospital. Not that we wanted to go to that awful town everybody talks about.

Later that night when Connie came up to bed I asked her to get us a drink of water because we were on fire and the jug was empty, but she only got one glassful.

"Where's mine, Connie?"

"That's yours. I didn't get one for . . . him. Dad says we aren't allowed to mention that boy's name anymore, let alone fetch and carry for him."

She was smug and for once I *did* hate her, and I was glad when Mum came in and heard and boxed her ears good and hard.

"Go to bed, Puss, and don't let me even hear your teeth chatter," Mum said. "When it's Show-poker Time in this house I'm the *really* Big Pig with the Real Big Hand. You remember that; I say who comes and goes in this zoo, and if you and your father aren't careful you'll both be out on your behinds."

It was cold and drizzly-shivery out, too, and the leaves

on the tree outside were tipper-tappering on the window
to wave good-bye to me before they died.

"Why do the leaves go away, Mum?"

"They only live for a year, darling. Then they die to
make way for all those new little green fingers that come
in the spring."

"Will Jack and me die now, Mummy, to make way for
other new little boys in the spring?"

"No. Not for a long time to come, baby. Not until
you've had children of your own and they've had children
and you've watched them grow up . . . and you've grown
tired."

"And *then* we'll die?"

"That's a long time away and your world will be old,"
Mum said.

"Like Granny?"

"Granny's not even that old yet."

"*She'll* never admit it!" Connie growled.

"Will you be here when we wake up, Mum?"

"I'll be right here where I am now."

"That's good."

I love Mum when she answers all my questions and
promises to be there. No shilly-shallying. If I said I was
going from Frisco to St. Jo and Mum promised to be there
when I got there . . . she *would be*. And even after I die, I
think Mum will be there wherever I open my eyes. And
when she tells Connie that she's the Really Big Pig with
the Real Big Hand when it's Show-poker Time, and uses
words like *Absolooly Imperative*, I feel safe . . . and me
and Jack snuggle up together and feel safe, as if all the
warm blankets in the world were wrapped around us.

"Keep warm, keep warm, Jackie!"

When Mum's there we know nothing in the world can
hurt us. Not Indians or Baddies or those Spacemen Connie

says are invading us. They wouldn't have a chance. Even
if those Forty Basstids with Forty-foot Poles that Dad's
always talking about came when Mum was all het-up she'd
give them all Paddy-whack-the-drumstick . . .

"Nance? You're crying."

"Tony."

"Don't cry. Fella'll be OK."

"But . . . I hit Connie."

"She'll forgive you. Connie forgets. Nothing matters
deeply to her unless it flies."

"Oh God, Antony. What must it be like to lose them?
To have them and baby them. Love them. Be a part of
them . . . and then lose them when they're still babies. How
do people survive such agony? I've never felt tears the way
I feel these tears tonight. And some of them for a little boy
. . . like Jack Rivers. Don't tell me I'm an idiot or you'll
shatter me completely."

"You're not stupid, honey. Just the best mother three
kids ever had."

Jack Rivers and me think about all these things when we
wake in the morning and just lie there wondering.

"You've got all the worries of the world in your holsters,
Boys," Mum said.

But we know there's always more sixpences in our Christmas pudding than in other people's pudding.

"You're a couple of silly nits," Connie said. "One day
you're gonna get caught in a fine tooth comb."

"Like you'd get caught pinching Dad's special cookies if
we didn't keep nitsy for you?"

"I could manage that alone anytime. I got more apples
in me head than Tasmania," Connie said.

"She could steal lead out of a pencil," Mum said.

"If she pinches any more of my cigarettes," Dad said, "I'm gonna get me some shares in W.D. & H.O. Wills."

Whoever they may be when the dominoes fall the wrong way. Jack and me, we wouldn't even pinch a baby.

"Such gentle boys," Mum said (again).

"They got more problems than you think," Connie said. "When we go to the Lake Park next summer they'll be too big to go to the Ladies' with you and too gentle to go to the Gents' by themselves."

"We'll cross that bridge when we come to it," Mum said, very very very very sweetly.

"Well, if it's made of sugar you might make it across without being noticed, Mother," Connie said, much more verily sweetly than Mum even. I tell you my sister is the one to watch out for in this town. She's . . .

"You're a little shit, Connie," Dad said. "Got guts . . . *but*."

5

THEY SAY a mighty gum fell hundreds of years ago where Main Road and Cambridge Street would some day attract each other and conceive Boomeroo. The townspeople like to believe that the name is composed of boomerang and kangaroo, and townspeople everywhere have this annoying habit of being right about such localisms and absurdities.

When this tree fell it had to be the highest thing on the valley slope, six times as girthy as Buddha and with all of thirty times as many arms as Vishnu.

"That tree musta been bigger round the gut than Big Fat Nellie because when she sits on the Death Seat there's room to spare."

"If you ain't got a sense of smell!"

The earliest Chadla timber cutters tried hauling this superb log away after they had undressed all the worthwhile and get-at-able timber on the Kaiser approaches; but their many and varied multibullocked attempts failed and they left it to the ferns and loping lianas. Desperate later, they became satisfied with haulable pieces from its massive length taken from spine-cracked places suffered in its fall.

Finally all that remained was the invincible root. A splendid semiextracted tooth of Nature: the end of possibly the most ancient iron-gum that ever reached for a piece of east Australian heaven. This heart and semblant soul of a fading forest would not rot and would not be called dead. It stayed on the spot where it had been a seed before Captain Phillip camped beside the Tank Stream: determined to outlive the men who had never known its true majesty but who had conquered its empire and stripped its skeleton. To prove itself unpetrified by man or time, each spring it threw out a classic rampant green arm, as bizarre as the oldest of traditions and as heraldic as any Royal Crest.

But finally some stubborn old timber cutter, admitting he was defeated and not minding, unhitched his cursed bullocks, pitched his tent beside it, boiled his billy and painted EMOH YM on a piece of bark.

When a few Welsh cousins visited this settled-down timber cutter and found coal in the vicinity, one factor was complete, because in those granddaddy days two tents made a street. This canvas camp became Main Road . . . Boomeroo. Other settlers had drifted up the valley on the south side of the creek after a gold rumour. Later still more came along with the sparrows, in the wake of the sleepers, when the railway came to Kincomba . . .

"I don't wanta talk about that place anymore," a heart-broken beer swiller said. "Not since I heard Goldie Killorn's goin'ta marry a Cucumber."

"Goldie wouldn't do that! She's a Boomerooster to the backside."

"OK down the front, too," Tony Delarue said.

"You grubs don't know anything," a half-pissed cement worker said, taking a chance that Tony wasn't drunk enough to object to being included among the grubs. "She's marryin' a joker from Sydney. He's only in Kincomba to take photographs of the valley for the *Women's Weekly* ... from all angles."

"Don't blame him for starting with Goldie. She's got the best angles in this neck o' the bush."

Goldie Killorn knew them better than they knew themselves in the pub.

"You'll have to come to Boomeroo before you definitely decide to marry me, Darcy," she said to her fiancé, "and find out what people say about me in my own back yard."

"Why? You told me about Ben Leslie. Small-town gossip wouldn't change my mind."

"I want you to understand the things I grew up with, just as I want to learn about your life in Sydney. The things that happened to you there, whether yesterday or in rompers."

"Rompers?" Darcy said.

"See?" Goldie said. "Different worlds. I don't even know how long you were in nappies."

"Goldie . . . baby, I have the world's laziest memory. I can't even remember when I first knew I was a boy."

"I doubt if you *could* cope with Boomeroo."

"That depends on my foolishness and your bravery, doesn't it?" Darcy said.

"And whether I give this watch back to Ben Leslie?"

"That's the only stipulation I've made."

"Make sure of me, Darcy," Goldie said. "This is not a trial run. We both did our apprenticeships before we met."

"OK, OK," Darcy said. "I promise."

"And you promised to go and photograph the Death Seat?"

"Oh . . . that," Darcy said, as though Kodacolor winds were blowing through his mind.

"Yes. That," Goldie said, as though nostalgia was in the present tense.

"I love you," Darcy said.

"I want you to love more than you see," Goldie said.

When the government decided to extend the railway north-west from Kincomba through the Booradeela Range to Walla Walla, the navvies building that line and digging the tunnel beneath the mountains on the other side of Dooragul Creek became Boomeroo's parental salvation. They came over to the shanties and fucked a town into existence. It was still referred to as Coal Creek, a place where miners ferried their coal across to a railway spur.

A rambling navvy-cum-explorer called Oxford discovered a route across the mountains on the north side of the creek, following his own flexible supposition that a bastard range such as the Booradeela — flung off from the Great Divide as it was — might strangely enough have its weakest point close to its highest. Boomeroo became heard of in the booming wake of the westward hopers.

The pathway from the first shanty on Main Road to the jetty opposite the rookery of navvy tents across the creek became Cambridge Street. The pass itself had to wait tiresome years until government channels ran dry of inappropriate suggestions, before it was officially named after its discoverer.

Young Cambridge Street got huskier and had to be widened in an effort to straighten it, for it had grown like a dog's hind leg. It was stepped out, measured off, squared off, laid out, thrashed over and finagled around in eighty-nine different directions. It was even given the pioneering benefit of a theodolite . . .

"That some kind of hermodolite?"

"You mean hermaphrodite, you grub!" . . . but there was

no escaping it: Right there at the perfect ninety-degree spot where Cambridge Street would meet Main Road was . . .

"The hermophodite?"

"Hermaphrodite, you fuckin' stupid grub." . . . *that bloody big root of that bloody big tree* . . . and there was no getting around the well-I'll-be-buggered thing. It was burnt into, dug at and chopped over without much noticeable success. Temporarily, the two streets met around the rotten unrotting stump.

One night it was moved slightly when an Irish navvy, rooted in rebellion and/or descended from Guy Fawkes . . .

"You can throw a leg over Billie Hawke's wife anytime. She's always home and she roots like a rebel." . . . pinched a pile of dynamite and exploded the lot beneath it. He swore the stump rose about two feet, puffed out a near-petrified fart and fell back right where it evidently intended to remain.

The glorious old gum root rested a few years on these horrific laurels until the day when a now-forgotten colonial Michelangelo had a brain bubble.

"Chisel the fucking thing," he said (*in Italian*).

The folks responded in a Babel of wretched growing-colony languages, well-raisined with London convict Cockney and Irish rigmarole, and . . . with their chisels. Big blunt and little sharp chisels. Shining iron and rusty ruined chisels. Or as some bush bard wrote:

> *Halves of chisels, crowbars of chisels,*
> *Infant chisels, old grand-chisels,*
> *Beautiful straight monogrammed*
> *And ugly unowned crippled chisels.*
> *Chisels that stuck, chisels that bounced,*
> *Chisels that crept, chisels that pounced.*
> *Borrowed chisels, stolen, dangerous;*

Chisels of friends with bevelled ends.
Double-ended and — handled chisels;
Fancy chisels, freak chisels.
Angry chisels, meek chisels.
Left-hand driven, right-hand riven.

"Sounds like masturbatin' chisels."
"Bi-chisels!"
"Hi-fi chisels!"
"Hermophodite chisels?"
Oh, come off it.
"The bloody blind with bloody braille chisels!"
Get stuffed.
"You mean get chiselled?"
The townspeople chiselled away at the tree trunk in their anger and fury. It became an addiction. Bad boys were made to and good girls were allowed to. Old men gnawed on the subject poetically, but basic old women pegged their pet parrots around it at night. It was more than an obsession: it was war. Until one day a strange and sudden thing happened: people quit trying to destroy that great and ugly forest relic and chose to adore it and restore it instead.

They say it was a Sunday when it happened and that would have helped keep the myth alive. Some say it happened in a fearful way amid panic. Others swear that it came about in simple silence. They say a lot of things about it, but Granfarver Jones was there ... and believedly the only person still alive ... so unfortunately he has to be accepted as the true authority. Sadly enough Granfarver tells it like it was in a different way every time he is asked to.

"As well as when he's not asked."
You can buttton your braces on that. You could say that,

like Mrs. Allsop, Granfarver Jones is immune to other people's imagination.

"If Mrs. Allsop finds out you mentioned her name in the same breff as Granfarver Jones she'll have your guts for garters."

"Now look here, Fay," Mrs. Allsop said to Fay Carrington, an um-time friend, her eyes as veined as Tuggeroo Wash at low tide when the mud was yellow as jaundice with the sulphur pollution from Boomeroo Cement Works, "we've been friends for a long time and you know I'm nothing if not outspoken."

If there had been such a word as *frienemies* Mrs. Allsop could have substituted it without changing tone.

"So . . . if I ever hear you talk about me in the same breath as that dirty old lizard, Granfarver Jones, whose BO is worse than a basketful of rotten mangoes, I'll bloody-well *wallop* you one."

She hitched her skirt at the same time as she lifted her throat, a sure sign that there were more things in heaven and on earth than Shakespeare ever dreamt about and that Fay was the next to hear them.

"That's like comparing *the Queen* to . . . Mr. Menzies! There are a lot of unpleasant things the Queen has to do . . . and she does them with a-plum. Like me when I have to put people like you on the right track. It isn't pleasant and I don't enjoy it." What a gorgeous lie! "But Bob Menzies . . . well . . . he only says things that make him sound clever . . . when all he ever does is wander round the halls of Canberra counting heads, and around the back passages of Buckingham Palace in his Garter gear, pulling chains for Royalty." Talk about a Royal Routine Flush! "On the other hand, as I'm trying to explain . . . me and the Queen only do and say what is necessary and imperative. For the best, so to speak, unpleasant or otherwise though it may be." A likely story. "We've got what it takes for such things. The Queen's got the upbringing and I've got the guts. But what have Granfarver Jones and Bob Menzies got?"

The Boomeroo Rugby Union Bulls could have made a scrum out of that sixty-four-cent question. But where is Granfarver Jones to tell us about the change in the attitude of the chisellers?

"Down the old Railway Pub. What the fuck you think we're all doin' drinkin' up here?"

6

THIS ROOM is a big room and this bed is a big bed, bigger than Connie's. The window is high, wide and handy for throwing Minties' wrappers out of. Mum said this is an enormous house and that's why we only use part of it. It was built by Samuel Oxford, who we come from, and a lot of other people *say* they come from . . . except the holy-rolling Joneses and their relations who are nearly everybody else in Boomeroo if you go back far enough . . . and please don't throw your Minties' wrappers out of the window, Boys.

But my Dad doesn't come from people, he comes from America. "I came here to get away from my family," Dad said. "I was sick of being up to the ass in relatives."

We live here because this old Oxford house now belongs to Mum, and that is supposed to prove she comes from Oxford . . .

"Right through the Pass," Dad said.

"Well, at least Leo didn't wait till she died before signing it over to me," Mum said. You see, Laura Eva Oxford's Dad used to call her Leo when she was a little girl.

"She's still a bloody old lion," Dad said.

Sometimes Connie tries to shake us out of bed if we're having our nap when she comes home from school, but we hang onto the bed-head like grim death because we love our bed. Isn't that a nice expression? Like Grim Death. Jack Rivers and me, we like most things to do with Death and we're dying to be old enough to sit on the Death Seat by ourselves. We also want to visit Death Valley that Dad often talks about.

"My gulp stream's as dry as Death Valley," Dad said, racing off to the Sulphide Hotel.

"There's nothing the matter with his legs," Mum said. "They know their own way to the pub."

The ceiling of the bedroom seems higher than Connie's kites fly and it scowls down at us. Mum says it's more like London Bridge when she has to pick up the plaster that frittles down. I must say, though, Jack and me have begun to notice that all these things are not as big as they used to be. That's funny, isn't it?

"When you're as big as me," Connie said, "you'll start to think you're livin' in a kennel."

Once I thought the ceiling was heaven and that I'd never reach it till I died. Now I think I'll be big enough to jump up and touch it (with a spring from the bed) by the time I'm ten and old enough to get my bike, if I don't die before then. Connie can scrape cobwebs from the corners by holding a broom high and bouncing up and down on her bed.

"I'll swipe that sick smile off those plaster angels' faces even if I cripple myself trying," Connie said.

"I'll have to do something about the ceiling in the kids' room," Dad said. "Those angels are falling faster than the girls in the Tenderloin."

"Where's the Tenderloin?" Connie said.

"Was a place in Li'l Ol' New York," Dad said. "But I

think there's one in Chadla run by one of the old Gay
Gordon Girls."

"*Antony!*" Mum said, like as if the sky was falling, not
the ceiling, and *that was that*.

Boy, is Mum a that-was-thatter!

The Gay Gordon Girls were Mrs. Allsop and her two
sisters, Rhondha (there's two aitches there somewhere)
Cornelia and Bella Jordon Gordon, before they got married.
Rhondha Cornelia married an American sailor and last
heard of was alive and swell and divorced and living in the
heart of something called rip-snortin' San Diego. Bella
Drew-Jordon Gordon was a war widow with a big home
in Chadla that was a house away from home for the Army
boys, and was doing very-well-thank-you. Mrs. Allsop had
once been Alice Arden Henrietta Gordon, and though she
married Reggie Allsop early in the piece it did not stop her
from being the grubs' Betty Grable during the war when
Reggie was overseas doin' his bit.

"When those three sisters got together at a party and
sang 'A Gordon for Me' they just meant they'd call the
baby Gordon," Upsa Downey said.

"They fucked like all the sheilas during the war," Gutsa
Mevinney said. "They just use'ta faint first."

"You Aussie girls sure were good to us American boys,"
Tony said to Nance with a big bloppy wink.

"That's all you were," Nance said. "Boys!"

The Gay Gordon Girls knew how to send their fair
indiscriminate share of Aussies and Yanks off to war like
men. Boys who had left their Mums with a packed lunch,
a caked toothbrush, a clean hankie and tears were able to
bid the Gay Gordons adieu like heroes with short tomor-
rows, which most of them were.

"Mrs. Allsop may be a gossip," Nance said, "but she's

respectable . . . and who's to question what anybody did during the war?"

Old Mumma (Mrs. Fergus Gordon) had given her daughters lots of advice, and one piece remained with them: "Go as far as you know the way home, girls. It's your life and what other people think is a lot of cheap macramé." And according to their intelligence and feminism, conscience and moralism, they stuck to Old Mumma's compass.

They all had lofty singing voices, and you only had to hear Mrs. Allsop singing "The Northern Lights of Old Aberdeen" to make you wish you had been born beneath the aurora borealis instead of the australis . . . not to mention the tears you'd be surprised to find on the summit of your cheek. And at New Year she sang "Auld Lang Syne" as though God were listening and the angels knew it was hogmanay. And in the chaotic throes of a kitchen tea at the School of Arts you'd hear her even if you were driving through Kincomba traffic in a square-top Buick with the windows wound up.

"I like her, I like her," Tony said to shut Nance up.

"She oughta be an engine driver," Connie said. "She's always puttin' someone on the right track."

"Connie, can't we ever have a conversation without you putting in your pennyworth?"

"Well, she never spends it any other way," Peanut chirped.

"Darling," Nance said, "that was very clever. You are getting to be my smart little man."

"Better than burnin' holes in pockets like your money," Connie said, giving her brother a sneaky elbow. "You've only got two eyes; one chocolate and one vanilla."

At night the dark chases the ceiling away but we don't like the dark and the way it creeps softly and slowly up the

walls and blacks out the little angels on the ceiling tenderloin. We don't mind the moonlight dark, but. At Sunday
School there's a big picture of Jesus standing in the moonlight dark, so I suppose when you die you go to live with
Him in that moonlighty darkness.

"Don't tell me Jack Rivers is afraid of the dark?" Connie
said.

"No! He just likes sunlight better. Doesn't everybody?"
Sometimes I have good answers.

"I couldn't speak for the ghost community," Connie said.
"Personally I think Kid Rivers is a chicken and will eventually end up in one of Mrs. Allsop's feather pillows at a
bazaar . . . or some side show doohickey at Kincomba
Show."

"Aw . . . Connie!"

"So why don't he go to Korea?"

"He's been there!"

"I bet! The chicken left when the war started. He did
arrive here about that time. If you showed him an axe and
went quawk-quawk you wouldn't see him for dust and
moulted feathers." She laughed like a jackass in a snake pit.
"Maddy Rivers . . . half chicken, half boy . . . the midway
wheat eater . . . chook-chook-chook-chook-chook!"

Sometimes I can't think of a scrap of a thing to answer
her back with. Not one bloomin' scrap. It's so . . .

"Frustrating," Mum said. "I know just how you feel at
times, baby."

At times there's absolooly nothing you can say to Connie.
Like when she went into her Mad Hatter's laugh just
because I said Jack and me were going to be Marching Girls
when we grew up. We like those Marching Girls in Lake
Park when they do their soldier drill.

"Yah-hahahahahahahahahaha-yah-hoo. Marching Girls
yet?"

"Leave the Boys alone, Connie," Mum said. "Peanut and Jack don't pick on your friend, Maggie Gordon."

"Maggie's all right," Connie said. "She's normal. You pinch her, she feels it and yells."

"That is enough," Mum said.

Yeah, my Mum's one of those enoughers too.

"Well, Maggie's a good mate at school," Connie said. "And besides . . ."

"I said enough, Connie," Mum said. "Maggie Gordon is as silly as a wheel without an axle. She's got a hurdy-gurdy mind. The only one in that family with any brains was Callie Gordon, and she left home. I wish you'd make friends with nice little girls."

"You've already got two nice little girls," Connie said.

"*Connie!*"

"There's one thing I hate about this family," Connie said. "Nobody wants to shut up unless they have the last word."

"So you've had it," Mum said.

"See what I mean?" Connie said.

"Callie Gordon went to London . . . that's what those skipping-rope girls sing," I said.

"Worst thing about Maggie," Connie said to us once, "is she's Duck Allsop's cousin."

"What's a cousin, Connie?"

"Someone you fight with, then your mothers fight because you did . . . because you're related."

"Where's our cousins?"

"We don't have any in Australia, thank God."

"Because I was an only child," Mum said. Mum listens to what's going on sometimes when you don't know it. You gotta be careful like that.

"You got ears like a radio telescope, Nance," Dad said. "Great-blazes-on-the-sun have you got ears!"

"Me and Clark Gable," Mum said.

"You've got fourteen cousins in Ame'ica," Dad said.

"Write me off their list for peace' sake," Connie said.

"Jack Rivers is an only child like Mum."

"I'm gonna chuck," Connie said. "I feel sicker than the day I swiped the Pavlova and vomited out the window all over those stupid skipping girls." Connie hates those skipping-rope girls . . . the ones Mum calls Nice Girls.

"Such nice, happy, well-dressed little girls," Mum said.

"They're the Stricken End!" Connie sounded like Dad talking about the fat laundrette ladies.

Those nice happy little girls skip out in the front of our shop while their mothers are waiting for their wash, yakking and bugging my dad.

They sing:

Callie Gordon went to London
On a great big white liner . . .
When she went to see the Queen,
The Queen had a beaut black shiner.

They have other songs. This is Jack's favourite:

Play with toys till you're old enough for boys . . .
Then let them play with you.
Play with rope till you're old enough to hope . . .
One of those boys will marry you.

"What drivel those skipping minnies sing!" Connie said. I love this one most:

Now Sally's married
She must be good
And help her husband
Chop the wood;
Bring it in
And light a fire
Then she'll be
His Heart's Desire.

"Catch me chopping some guy's firewood! If he can't light my fire to hell with him," Connie said.

"What's a Heart's Desire, Connie?"

"A lot of love shit! A guy gets a licence to marry you and own you the same as he does to drive a car or have a wireless."

I suppose Connie's hot enough: she's always fuming over something. I tell you something, but; if Saul Hamilton ever lights her fire it's gonna be like a bushfire in January when it hasn't rained for forty weeks and those Forty Basstids with Forty-foot Poles are drier than alum. Whatever that is.

"I'm drier than flamin' Moses eatin' alum," Dad said. "And he was in the desert for Forty Days and Forty Nights without a drink; and Forty Basstids with Forty-foot Poles tryin' to break all the Commandments in Forty Minutes." Dad sure loves the forties.

"I think you got Moses and Someone Else mixed up, Dad," Connie said.

The worst thing you can do to Connie is to look in her dressing-table drawers because that's where all her Glorious Loot is. (Connie's always bringing home this secret Glorious Loot.) Trouble is those drawers are slippery and pop right out sometimes as easily as Dad's teeth, but they make more mess. Dad keeps his teeth in a glass of water at night and nobody better even grin back at them. If Connie catches us at her drawers she's like a dog in a flea circus. We try to be quiet but sometimes the silence gives you away quicker than noise.

"And what, *pray*, are You Two Sneaks doing at my dresser?" Standing in the doorway with her hands on her hips, Connie makes us feel like a couple of worn-out Teddy Bears — the ones she buried alive a few years ago . . . or did she hang them first? I truly forget.

"Just lookin' at your Glorious Loot, Connie."

"You're looking for Trouble!" And that's what we get, Trouble with a T bigger than the big teapot they use at kitchen teas in the School of Arts.

"Well, put all that stuff back, and look out if I catch you there One More Time," Connie said. One More Time is probably more stricken than the Stricken End.

"Do you ever steal any of this Glorious Loot?"

"Watch it, imbo!"

"What *is* an imbo, Connie? Please?"

"If you don't know what imbeciles are far be it from me to tell you," Connie said. "Say . . . lookit the spider I put in that bottle last year. Seems like the poor critter's starved to death. That's life!"

"Can we have it now?"

"No. When you clean up that mess, go down and feed it to Froggo; and untie all the knots from my kite cord, and I'll let you off the hook this time."

What a relief. Connie's hooks are mighty big hooks. "Froggo's always hungry, isn't he?"

"He's so big and fat and ugly, and useless, I might have to get rid of him," Connie said. "Heck, if I was a hungry greedy frog I'd hang around an anthill or picket a beehive. He's stupid."

"What's a picket, Connie?"

"Someone too lazy to work for the money they already get at the pit because they've got too much money for beer."

"But Froggo don't drink beer."

"Oh, you're a nineteen-bob nut," Connie said. "Now do as I said; and get yourself out of here unless you want to end up red 'n' black. I'm gonna empty all the scent outa these bottles and make meself some ink from these inkberries. I wish Leo would remember I'm not a pretty-ninny with flaxen hair and quit sending me scent. Why doesn't she send me something I can use, like an old pair of corsets for wing frames . . . I can work miracles with those things." She can, too.

"We ask her for things we want most."

"Grandmas like boys best," Connie said. "When the wood's in and the coal's on the fire, it's true: Grandmas go for boys insteada girls."

"Why, Connie?"

"Because grandmas are a breed of their own and make their own rules and regulations. But Leo better start paying some attention to my wants . . . or else."

I can't bear to think of a Connie Or-else.

"Leo loves you, Connie," Mum said. "When you were little and cried a lot . . ."

"I get it, I get it," Connie said. "Spare me the sound effects."

". . . and I used to get angry with you, Leo said to me: 'Now Nance, babies can only let you know by crying or laughing what's the matter with them. You don't go on when she's laughing so why be cranky when she cries to tell you she's unhappy. Find out why or let me have her to nurse and cheer up.'"

"So she can make me happy now," Connie said, "just by sending me her old corsets. No nursing!"

Jack and me don't have a dressing table but we do have a wardrobe that Mum calls a lowboy. Isn't it a cute name for a wardrobe for little boys? We can open and close its doors as easy as going to the lavvie. We don't use potty anymore. Mum said she never even had to buy a lot of nappies. Connie sniggers and says she knows why, then swaggers about like Dad and shouts: "He'll shit on the pot, or else! Diapers are dirty things."

But I don't want to think about that.

Our lowboy is painted blue inside, where our coats and suits and shirts hang. Underneath are these little racks where our shoes sit, like a lot of black and brown teeth.

"Like Connie's will be soon if she doesn't brush more often," Mum said.

Jack and me use our toothbrush after every meal: Dad used to be a stickler for that but met his match in Connie and gave up. Jack and me and Mum will never meet our matches that way: we get on too well together.

"Like pukey calves," Connie said. "Mum rattles the bucket and You Two Milksops run to her."

That was the day she locked us in her wardrobe, which is too big for the room, really. Mum said.

Connie *knew* we were hiding there, but said it was an accident. Jack managed to get out and galloped downstairs to tell Mum of my Perdicament. I must say he took a long time and I did a lot of yelling and thumping in the meantime.

Connie copped the lot that day from both Mum and Dad for a change. Mum said it was an utter foolish thing for a sister to do and not becoming of a Fifth Class girl. Dad agreed for once (that maybe it wasn't an accident) and paddled Connie's butt.

"Connie, why is it when you're bad Dad paddles your butt, but when I'm naughty Mum says she'll larrup me? Not that she does."

"Same difference, you dobber!" Connie said. "Just wait till you're a bit older; you'll catch those flying fingers round your ass one day. Dad's got a mean whack when he's riled."

"But I belong to Mum: she said she had me, so Dad must've had you."

"You're so dumb," Connie said, "you don't even know what's what in Murrungarot and who's who in Boomeroo."

"You're not a very truly friend, Connie."

"And you're lousy with adjectives and adverbs," Connie said. "Wait till you get in Miss Bowen's class at school. She's got this big thing about adverbs and adjectives. Like as if they were important."

"We're *your friends*, Connie."

"Any more friends like you and I'd go to Korea," Connie said. "Dobbing me in. I was just trying to get you used to the dark in that wardrobe."

Connie can get round anything.

I think the very best next friend to Mum is the tree on the footpath outside our window. Oh, by the way, Dad calls the footpath a sidewalk and Leo calls it a pavement. Honest, I don't know why. Dad says a lot of things we have to ask about at times. Mum explains mostly . . . unless it's rude. Dad called somebody a dirty cocksucker once.

"Mum? What's a dirty cocksu . . ."

"Dad's being rude again. Pay no attention to him."

There's no two ways about it, we spend a lot of time trying to figure out the difference between what Mum says and what Dad means and how Connie explains it all.

"Where's me dungarees?"

"You can't wear slacks to Sunday School, Connie."

"Oh, let her wear them, Nance. She looks good in jeans."

"Jack and me wear pants, Mum."

"Yes. You Two look lovely in your grey Sunday suits," Mum said, "but girls who . . ."

"Drop their dacks come home screw-loose," Dad said.

"Stick to your Funnies, funny man," Mum said to Dad. She meant the comics.

"What *are* dacks, Connie?" I asked on the way to Sunday School.

"Something men and women drop before they screw," Connie said.

"But wouldn't a screwdriver be . . ."

"Forget it for a few more years," Connie said. "Lots of words have two meanings, Peanut. You'll be sure of what you're saying by that time . . . I hope to God."

"Like when I get my two-wheeler bike?"

"Like when you get your bike."

"Then I can use screw words?"

"Check with me first," Connie said. "The world's turning in more ways than one, you know. And things and words keep turning and changing. There might be a better word to use by the time you're ten."

"Will there be better things to do than screw when I'm ten and have my bike, too, Connie?"

"Oh, screw you and your bike," Connie said. "We might all be dead by then."

"Yes, I know. I'm always telling Mum that, but she don't want to hear it no more."

"Oh . . . you . . . child."

Connie must have remembered it was Sunday. She can be so nice at times.

7

A PUB IS A PUB is a pub. Not so. A hotel in Boomeroo
is a shrine, the holy local. The power of the pub is divinity
in two languages: bad and filthy. In the late forties and
early fifties the country bars were still usually sexually
limited. In the cities women and lesbians drank in the bars
and ladies lingered or lolled in the lounges; but in country
towns the grubs and molls met only in the saloons . . .
ladies drank at home, seething, waiting for liberation.

When dissected in the most popular pub, the Sulphide
Hotel — where everything alive and sick and grubbing in
Boomeroo was eventually anatomized — the town itself
was eight blocks long by four blocks wide, give or take a
misplaced gutter.

"Five if ya count Creek Street."

"How would you know, you prick? Y've only got four
fingers, and you're too busy pullin' it to count on them . . .
so shut up and shout!"

The shorter streets were called after colleges and universities . . . sort of. There was University, Church, Cambridge, Scots, Harrow, Radley . . .

"That's a place near Oxford. In England."

"I know where Oxford fuckin' is. So why haven't we got a fuckin' Oxford Street?"

"Because Oxford was a modest bastard, you lippy cunt."

. . . I repeat Radley, Kings and finally Harvard.

"Bloody Yankee college."

"We should have a Rugby Street. Everyone round here plays Rugby Union."

The longer streets were Main, High, and Pacific Avenue embellishing the rising grade of the town.

Reserve Terrace was parallel to these streets, below Main, and was hemmed by the north bank of Dooragul Creek where it flushed Boomeroo.

"Boomeroo's a bit laid out like New York from what I know and see in the movies."

"Then you know fuck-all. It's more laid out like Letty Conway, an' she got hit by the shit lorry ten years ago."

Creek Street was on the south bank of the Dooragul and was electorally in Wollondonga.

Bora Bora and Chadla were the only other towns of a valuable size on the Dooragul northside, and the maze of wandering coal-train tracks interlaid in the triangle between these two towns and Boomeroo probably boggled the eyes of many an earnest homing pigeon.

Apart from a cupboardlike wine bar at the corner of Main Road and Kings Street — where old ladies drank plonk for a shilling a shot and had their teacups read for two-and-six — there were four hotels.

The Kraigee Hotel, a modern roadside hostel, was the only postwar drinking spot. It was built of MacDonald Mountain stone on the strength of a licence that belonged to a once flourishing Minmi pub. It was beyond Harvard

Street on Main Road but *this* side of the Rexona billboard, so it was within the town limits. It was also known as the Kraigee Cuntery because there was more than beer laid on there.

The Railway Hotel was across the street from Boomeroo railway station. It was Granfarver Jones's hangout, so not very popular with the young bucks who had heard his stories more times than they had jacked off in their school days.

"The old bastard earbashes travelling salesmen and visitors now."

His most popular tale was still the one about Yellow Long, Thunderbolt's mistress . . . of how in a jealous rage, she throttled the strumpet, Biddy Conway, and dumped her body in the deep springs in the shadow on Mount Kaiser.

"Amen! Hands up anybody who hasn't heard that one about fifty fuckin' waltzin' times?"

The two pubs that mattered most to the men of Boomeroo were the Commercial where the miners and overalled tradesmen and the sixteen- and seventeen-year-olds drank . . .

"Fifteen if ya dirty and on ya way home from work!"

"Well, wha's'use of leavin' school to work if ya can't go to the pub?"

. . . and the Sulphide where the cement workers, footballers and small businessmen unwound with middies and schooners, and on festive occasions with pints.

The Commercial was one of those brewery-owned pubs that changed facades with the decades. Originally it had been bastard colonial. For a time during the Great War it was Frenchified with canvas and five poplars. The trees had defied future changes and were still there, immense and shady in summer, beautifully bare-boned in winter.

In the twenties it was given a California-Spanish stucco face-lift.

"What about the speakeasy look they gave the saloon before the Depression? When the molls used to wear their garters showin'."

"How would you know, pinhead? You were so bloody young your prick musta been the size of a .22 short."

"It's still only about the size of a .22 long."

In the thirties it was tiled pink in front and looked like a big Hollywood bathroom.

"All it needed was Jean Harlow in the raw."

The forties saw it timbered back and sides by some lumber barber . . . barred, buffered, raftered and accented with dung-coloured, slop-stained second-grade pine.

Recently, it had been stripped to its rough brick spine, chipped and air blasted. Its red and pink and slate brick skeletal beauty was radiant even in the rain; and there were plans for the best-bloody-beer-garden on the northside of the creek. On dry windy days when the town was chapped and disfigured a misty yellow as the sulphur from the Cement Works stirred around it, the Commercial and its gently bending poplars were the only gorgeous phantoms in town.

The Sulphide Hotel had been built in 1892. It had been reroofed once since then and repainted a few times and that was all.

" 'Cept they moved the shithouse closer to the back of the pub when we got the sewer."

The huge mahogany mantelpieces at each end of the long mahogany bar were terrifying, wondrous, hand-carved, undusted monsters. The bar itself was polished in the history of thousands and thousands of cold and dripping beer glasses, and shone like a mirage on hot, soft black asphalt. The mighty cedar shelves at the back of the bar were like jury boxes filled with unheard-from exotic bottles, and the mirrors they encased frost-eyed witnesses of measureless incidental crimes.

"I tried that there Dom once. It tasted like cocker-roach piss. Me cattle-dog lapped it up, but!"

"Holy Mackerel . . . don't ever try that Napoleon choir-someth'n-or-other. Been there since Samson had long hair."

The old oil-lamp fittings, the remaining spittoons, door plates and knobs, bar braces and window grips, ungilded paintings in disjointed frames that still clawed at the webbed walls, and the porcelain graveyard pieces enshrined above the giant fireplaces, were unknowingly priceless. The few crippled chairs and tables, the fire tongs and pokers, the moulded glass ashtrays that bounced and most of the older (non-Union) glasses were what they looked like . . . Early Hockshop. The inch-and-a-half floorboards were heel- and toe-carved, and where they butted the bar below the brass foot rail there were places you could spit through to the rubbish below if you were straight enough.

"But for Chrissake throw your butts in the spittoons not down there or you'll singe the cattle dogs restin' underneath in the shade."

The rolled edge of the bar where elbows had rubbed and been raised lovingly in mateship for over half a century was smoother than a virgin's stomach and warmer than a mother's cheek . . . and, oh, save me from perdition, the beer was brilliant. This was the true pulpit of Boomeroo where any man could preach anything . . .

"We can stick to our idiot . . . sincrasses if we wanta."

. . . for this was early Australiana appendixed, and sooner or later every edict and verdict affecting the town was by-fucked across this magistral bar.

The ministering licensee, born on the premises, was the daughter of the original owner. Molly Cowmeadow (pronounced Carmody) ran the business with the help of a couple of sister barmaids as crone as herself, Missy and Ginger (what else?) Meggs, and an ageless son. This boy-man . . .

"Jason's got a prick all right, but you can only see it on a clear day: looks a bit like a witchetty grub."

. . . of little brawn and less brain but as big as an epicene elephant, merely went into action by dominated mechanical reflexes when any one of those three old boilers yelled for anything . . . from a toilet roll to a fresh keg.

Here was the other side of the Death Seat's magnetism which relied upon the introspective massaging of love. The pull of this pub, for all its earthiness, had more to do with the arrogance of hate: hating most what they did not want to accept or understand.

"Aw, come off it! What do you mean by *hate*? Little Grub, here, is the most underhated man in town. Don't mean anybody loves him."

"Bog is the most hated man on the Chadla Racecourse, but everybody loves him when he's here." Bog, Bob O'Grady, ran a crook book.

Everybody in this pub hated somebody, and firmly believed any close relationship between any man and woman ended up in some concession to hate.

"Not between mates, but!"

"An' we all love Pinhead. He's too dirty to fuck and too crazy to hate."

The Death Seat is intimate medicine: the Sulphide Pub is an easily available, fast, free prescription. The Death Seat's true arsenal is the catenation of faith kept deep in the souls of men, assessing them from link to link, dividing them from the apes.

If you left this town, this valley, this pub, and found yourself adrift in some strange world, knowing you would never see this place again, wouldn't your heart abandon you?

"What would you do, mate?"

"First I'd have a nice long uncomplicated piss, then I'd try their beer. Four blacks, Molly!"

There are a few things the Death Seat can't cope with and the pub can't arbitrate on.

"Wish I was young and ready for Eternity Smith again."

"She pays more money than ever now for a blowjob."

"She could inflate me any time."

"Gives the young guys five quid now, I hear."

"Pays on the dot!"

"Sure beats inflation . . . where they promise you a raise at the Cement Works next month and everything in the Store went up last month."

Mrs. Evelyn Hendon Smith was a wealthy, roaming evangelist who spent six months of the year on the north central coast of the state. She rented the School of Arts in Boomeroo for a week and stayed at the Kraigee. Her services were full of the promise of eternity for those who gave up their sinful ways and had tea and bickies with her after the sermon. But she never gave her real secret away, and the women went home damning her for being about eighty and looking a young sixty.

The men knew. As youngsters more than half of them had helped her revitalize herself.

"That's what she calls it . . . revitalization."

"What she does and does well is give you a bloody good old gamarouche . . . and pays you."

"Swallows the whole friggin' load."

"Young Henry Garside said she nearly reefed his bloody prick off."

Not quite true. Poor old Eternity couldn't get her throat free of Young Henry's unbelievably enormous cock and was choking to death.

She was also generally accessible on summer Sundays in her colourful canvas headquarters at Lake Park, and the growing boys looked forward to when they were sixteen and old enough (above carnal untouchability) to service Eternity. The old moll was not only a stickler for fellatio but also for procedure. The first time she used a young stud she insisted upon seeing his birth certificate.

"No fuckin' around! You give her a heavy wad or you'll never make it to her tent flap again."

" 'Ow do you get onto 'er?"

" 'S'easy, son. Go to one of 'er sermons, wearin' a clean white shirt, *no underpants*, polished shoes and wiff your birff certificate stickin' outa your pocket. If you throw a good load she'll keep you on tillya nineteen."

"The amount of spoof is more important to Eternity than the size of your cock. She's polite about that."

It was a waste of time tigering for favours. Boys with speedwell blue eyes and God-bodlike rods were no more welcome than ugly duck-bum little bastards. She swallowed the flood of their youthful passion, licked the dribbles from their soft-haired balls, slapped five quid into their emotion-clenched hands and said, "Thank you, dear. Come back when you're loaded again." And helped them pull their rumpled pants up from around their shivering ankles.

"I'd really like to know that old bitch's secret as well as her real age, Bertha," Mrs. Allsop said to a bewildered friendly Eternity-hater. "I'd give quids and flesh to know. She's eighty if she's a year and not a line on her sinful face."

The very young were curious, too.

"How do you spell gamarouche?" Batter Rees said.

"I don't know. I looked in me best dictionary but it ain't even in that," Monte Howard said.

"What *exactly* is it?" Gloamie Lightfoot said.

"She gobbles you off. What Mr. Delarue calls a blow-job," Swiftie Madison said.

"You gotta let 'er swallow all ya come."

"*BeJeseeeesus!*"

"Wish I was sixteen."

"And she gives you money?"

"*Five . . . beautiful . . . fuckin' . . . quid.*"

Nobody needs money the way you need money when you're sixteen, seventeen and eighteen. And nobody needs dreams and ambitions so much when they're old as when they're young.

"I still dream of marrying Goldie Killorn, even if she is engaged," Monte said. "She was down our street to see Jerry Kyle last week."

"Hi," Goldie said to Jerry. "Your Mum home?"

"Not at the moment." Jerry's voice squinted as much as his face.

"Well, it *was* you I wanted to see," Goldie said. "To ask you if you'd sing at my wedding."

"Do you think I'm good enough?"

"You're still the only one I hear in the choir. Will you ask your mum?"

"Oh, it'll be OK, Miss Killorn, I'd love to. I'm glad you asked me."

"It's a nice piece called 'Bless Every Hour,'" Goldie said, with a smile he figured blessed him.

"If you leave the music sheet with Miss Frederickson I can practise with her after Sunday School," Jerry said.

"You're a good kid."

Jerry looked as inspired as if he had just been told God had created another world in five days. The onlooker, Monte Howard, remained entirely speechless for the first time in his life.

"So . . . I'd better scoot," Goldie said, "and let you boys get on with whatever it was . . . you were doing. Hi, Monte . . . cat give you a scare?"

Monte shook his head. "No. No, Miss Killorn. I was just goin' . . . inside to . . ."

. . . whank off with that picture of you on the cover of the *Women's Weekly*. To hell with any eternity. I can grow up tomorrow.

8

NOBODY ELSE we know talks like my dad. Connie does sometimes but Mum says that's only when she's trying to get-Dad-in. I guess it must be all to do with my dad being a Yank. Did I tell you he was a Yank? Once he didn't like being called a Yank.

"Yankee, maybe. By Southerners, maybe," Dad said. "But Yank. Sounds like I spend my life whopping off."

Mum explained something or other to him and now he doesn't mind so much. Maybe he doesn't mind spending his time whopping off now, after all . . . whatever that may be.

"You mean it puts me in the good-old-bastard brotherhood?" Dad said.

"That should suit you," Mum said. "You love to be popular."

That's true. Dad loves to be popular. He goes out of his way to be popular . . .

"Dad would walk to Bourke with his legs tied behind his back just to keep popular," Connie said. Except when he's looped and then he goes out of his way looking for a fight. Sometimes when he's been to the pub on a Friday night longer than usual (and usual is long enough) he calls himself Yankee-doodle-doo, the best goddamn fighter in Boomer-oomer-oooo!

"Antony, you're drunk," Mum says.

Connie told me a Yankee was a man who fights South-erners, but I don't know what a Southerner is: they must all come out on Friday night, but, because that's Dad's fighting night out. I love him a lot even if he spends Friday nights fighting and the rest of his life whopping off. That must be something Yanks do best.

This morning the branches of Old Tree have more tiny leaves on them. We started counting these leaves a few days ago when they came back after winter and autumn.

"The fall," Dad said.

"The foll," Connie said, imitating him.

Mum laughed. "You pair sound like Professor Higgins and Eliza Doolittle. Talk about the rain in Spain being a pain!"

"That reminds me, Connie," Dad said. "Where I come from, when it rains we put our slickers on, not raincoats."

"Slicker," Connie said. "Great! Next foll I'll wear my slicker to scholl." They laughed at that.

Mum recited something to annoy them:

"*The fall in Gaul stalled all*
And Caesar called a halt . . .
But . . . when the foll in Goll stolled oll
Caesar called a holt!"

"Bolls," Dad said, and sang a Friday-night song:

"*Goin' back to old Oh-high-oh*
And spend my Friday nights . . .
In To-lead-oh."

"We'd all be better off if you'd never left *Hoh-hoh-hoh*," Mum said, slapping his supper in front of him as if he certainly wasn't in Boomeroo.

Best thing about Friday nights, we get to stay up late waiting for Dad to come home. "Six o'clock closing is getting closer to midnight every night," Mum said.

Just the same, I like the quiet mornings better than the wild nights. We counted the leaves until we got to eleven. That's easy because you've got ten fingers and the next one rhymes with heaven. Mum said so.

"Heaven's where you go when you die, isn't it?"

"That's right," Mum said.

"Guess it won't be long before me and Jackie go to heaven. Everything's piling up."

"Peanut, forget about dying today. Nothing's piling up except the housework."

"Connie said the world's piling up, Mum."

"Connie's a pile of gumbo."

We knew what she meant. Dad has a room at the back of the laundrette where he keeps all his junk, and we call it his gumbo room. Dad is not only a Yank who wants to be popular but he's also a hoarder. Wonder if he steals any of it like Connie?

"A rabid hoarder," Mum said; but me and Jack have never seen any rabbits in his gumbo room.

When the sun is on Old Tree it looks like a bit of coral Dad brought back from a place called the Islands, long before we came from Wherever. I'm sure I don't know where the Islands are but I don't think I came from there. I don't know where Wherever is either.

"For someone whose best friend knows everything you don't know much," Connie said.

"You don't know many tunes today, Connie?" Mum told us to say that one.

Through the tree-branchy coral we see scraps of blue sky that look like water, so we pretend that any minute now a few cloudy fishes will swim by.

"You boys have glad imaginations," Mum said.

"Polly and Anna," Connie said.

"Watch it, Connie!" Mum said.

"Cloud fish, indeed," Connie said.

"There are sunfish," Mum said, quick as that bird that sounds like a whip crack. Wouldn't we love to be that quick?

"Well . . . they sound like Kindie-kids. Run fish, run, here comes the sun, fish," Connie said. "Boy, if I was a fish and heard Those Two talking about me I'd ask a shark to have me for breakfast." She pounded out mimicking us. "Swim, fish, swim, here comes a dirty big bream. Yuk, fish, yuk, I think I'm gonna chuck. They're growing up sounding like a gramophone . . . and to think My Own Mother is winding up the machine."

Will you just listen to those chooks crowing, making a rooster racket! We like listening to the early morning noises. The milko running backwards and forwards across the street as if he was trying to get away from the daylight beginning to bounce his shadow around. The paper boy whish-whishing his papers.

We pretend the milko is making music to wake people up with his busy feet and grumbly stop-starting engine.

> *Brrr-stop, pitter pitter patter,*
> *Clink-clink-clink, wake up Mr. Kelly.*
> *Brrr-start, chugga-chugga-chugga;*
> *This is for you, Mrs. Delarue . . .*
> *And here it comes, Mrs. Nellie Thrums.*

That's Big Fat Nellie's proper name: bet you *didn't* know that. That rude paper boy, Duck Allsop, isn't musicky at all. He sounds more like a mad dog chasing Forty Basstids with Forty-foot Poles after Forty Screaming Cats; but we still like listening to him in the morning.

He's a tough nut and mighty mean, and dirty as his dirty big black retriever in winter . . . it goes swimming with all the nuddy boys in summer. He carries on like a larrikin with the rabies but we still try to sing to his bombing noises when he hoists his papers here and there.

> *Whish-whish . . . one for ya guts.*
> *Tingaling . . . belt hell outa this thing.*
> *Whish-whish, that'll cripple ya dog!*
> *Feroooompheroooom. Bloody-shit-I-missed!*
> *Tingaling . . . cop that in your gauze door.*
> *Keep behind me, you dirty big bloody*
> *Great black retriever, or I'll ram a*
> *Bike pedal up ya dirty big black arse!*

It isn't easy for us to sing to, so the birds wouldn't have a chance; besides they're too busy trying to miss the papers that fly sky-high.

"At least he earns his own pocket money," Mum said to Connie.

"He's a lousy fighter," Connie said.

"He's a cheeky young basstid," Dad said. "The only good thing he did was cramp old Pocket-penis Rowlandson's passion for paper boys."

"Antony!" Mum said.

Dad whispered something to her and she went quite pale and said, "It's a wonder the poor old man didn't bleed to death."

"Yeah, well, Duck's not very bright," Dad said, "but he sure must have strong teeth."

I don't know what Duck Allsop did to old Pocket-pennies Rowlandson but he did steal Jack Rivers's money box once.

"It's becoming a saga," Mum said.

You see Grandma Leo sent us these three little stools with a slot on top to put money in. There were palm trees painted on one side and a poem on the other and they were called souvenirs because they came from New Guinea and were made by men called Boys. The words on Jack Rivers's money box went like this:

> *Jack Rivers is no fool,*
> *He puts his pennies in his stool.*

Well, we had them in the back yard one day — I'm not just saying this but I have to admit it — and Jack forgot to bring his inside later. Connie's is never outside: she keeps hers under lock and key and a house brick in the bottom of her whopping great wardrobe.

"It would take Oxford himself the best part of a fortnight to find Connie's money box," Mum said.

"What the Sam Hill is a fortnight?" Dad said like he always does when that word is mentioned.

And Mum always ignores that one.

"Connie's economical," Dad said.

"She's mean, and it's a big failing," Mum said.

Connie *is* mean and it's one of her biggest failings and she has a lot of big fails. It would be more than the Tooth Fairy's wings were worth to leave That Miss less than sixpence under the tooth brick in the kitchen. When she was littler and losing teeth like I lose socks Mum said she used to even leave a note for the Tooth Fairy: *I want Big Money!* Why, she even comes to the barbershop with me and Dad just to get a penny back instead of going to the ladies' hairdresser with Mum. Me and Jack would like to go with Mum sometime and sit under those huge helmets even if we didn't get a penny back.

"Connie's still got the dime God gave her for spendin' money on the way from heaven," Dad said.

"I haven't got the dime God gave me, Dad," I said.

"Remind me to give it to you next Friday in that case," Dad said. One thing about the drink, it makes Dad generous on Fridays even if he is fighting fit.

"Could you give Jack Rivers and me a dime to spend on the way back to heaven instead, Dad?"

"Now what the hell you mean by that, kiddo?"

"Don't we go back to heaven when we die?"

"Listen, Fella, we don't die in this family," Dad said, tossing my hair. "We go to a better place . . . Ame'ica."

"Dadadadadadadadah," Mum sang.

Now this day Jack left his money box outside Duck Allsop happened to be at the laundrette horsin' around while he waited for his mother's clothes.

"She don't tub much, Mrs. Allsop," Dad said.

The next day, after the money box had . . . miser . . . myster . . . ably disappeared . . .

"A Real Catasterphe for a little boy," Mum said.

. . . Connie went to work.

Duck Allsop was getting round school spending money at the tuck-shop like as if he owned the Minties factory, and singing:

"Jack Rivers, the drongo fool . . .
Lost his dough when he lost his stool."

"He was spending pennies like he had holes in his hands," Connie said.

"My Jack's pennies!" I cried.

Mum told Dad not to go to Constable Hervey, because Jack Rivers wouldn't stand up in court if it got that far, and might be a laughing stock. I'm sure I don't know why. For once Dad agreed with her completely. Not that they fight a lot.

"They're parents," Connie said. "They have to have a go at each other now and then to prove they're married."

I told Mum Jack could share my money box, so she painted over my poem and printed on it:

Peanut and Jack are very wise,
They share their money and their lives.

Now . . . listen to this . . . a few days later Connie and her mates ganged up on Duck and bashed him up: even his cousin, Maggie Gordon, got in on the act.

"We caught him after school," Connie said. "Down the back in the little shed where the Infants have their play lunch. We cornered him there because he goes there to sneak a look at the girls in the lavatory on the other side of the wall. We surrounded him. We threw red inkberry ink in his face. It looked like blood and got our blood lust up. We battered him with our school bags till our arms were sore and there was real bloody *blood* flowing. *His not ours.*"

"Gee, Connie. Real blood?"

"You wanna hear or you wanna go paint your own picture?"

"We want to hear, Connie! We want to hear everything that happened to that . . . thief!"

"Then we had him on the ground. Wow! Long Sally Walker and Fat Phyllis Burroughs grabbed him by the legs and Sindelle Simpson held his hands while Big Myrtle Worthington sat on his belly. *Hah!* Did he scream when his guts popped like a corked-up bottle in a fire! Then Maggie Gordon beat shit outa his face: she was like a mad thing and sorta drove me on. The more she worked him over the more I pulled and tugged at him. It was like as if we were all trying to tear a piece outa his crouched-up body. Big Myrt took his dick out and spat on it. Sindelle was biting his arm and Long Sally and Fat Phyllis were scratching where it was soft inside his legs. But Maggie got uncontrollable and started putting the boot in, so we had to hold her off. After all, cousins aren't supposed to kill each other . . . 'cept in Civil Wars!' "

The way Connie told it I began to feel sorry for Duck Allsop even if he did steal Jackie's money box. It sounded like Korea. When she's got the Blood Lust Connie grinds on like Mum's anticky magic lantern. You can't help watching her . . . her eyes flicker and her mouth jiggles. I bet if we'd sent Big Myrt, Long Sally, Fat Phyllis, Mad Maggie and Sinderella Simpson to Korea those Chinks would've given up in no time. Hope I never have to face those girls with their Blood Lusts up.

"Duck loved every minute of the shinding . . . I think," Connie said, puzzled.

"Big Sister loved her Blood Lust Doctors on the wireless, Connie . . . and so did Mum."

"That poor bitch!" Dad said. "They've taken enough vital parts out 'f Big Sister to restore Forty Basstids to life. Everything except her last supper, and I guess they're savin' that for Christ's comeback."

"Antony, that is *enough*," Mum said; and I guess it was.

A few nights later I had a nightmare. It was really the blue divils! Those girls were charging up a hill in Korea with their Blood Lusts up, leading Forty Basstids with Forty-foot Poles . . . enough to scare Dracula. They surrounded Duck Allsop and Big Sister and a few slow Koreans, threw inkwell blood all over them and bashed shit out of them with forty-six school bags. Their Blood Lusts was . . . were something . . . grrrrlushious.

Then the Forty Basstids started fighting over the choice vital parts of Big Sister so The Girls ganged up on them. The rest was true horrible. A Real Catasterphe if I never use that word again. And wouldn't you know, Jack Rivers and me just happened to be riding by on Duck Allsop's dirty big black retriever. It made a pretty good horse, too.

When Mad Maggie saw me she wanted some of my vital parts because she'd missed out on the Big Sister parts. She missed out on me too, thank heavens, because as she rushed at me with her Blood Lust up and her eyes lit like the Store on Friday night I woke up yelling: "Not the Blood Lust! Not the Blood Lust!"

Next thing I knew Mum was stroking my forehead and saying, "It's all right, darling. You've had a bad dream. Go back to sleep. Mum's here."

"Mum . . . it was a real saga, you know? But, I'd feel better if we could have a midnight snack right now."

"I'm sure you would," Mum said with an ice cream smile. That's funny about me: unless I have something real important on my mind, like dying, I have ice cream and lollies on my mind.

"That little sonofabitch only has two things on his mind," Dad said. "Jack Rivers and ice cream."

"And licorice and black jelly beans," Connie said, as if she knew more than anybody else knew.

"Mum, I nearly died in Korea tonight. If you die in a dream is it for real? Or do you still wake up?"

"Dreams are not real," Mum said. "You're safe now. That's what matters."

"Mum . . . if I was the last to arrive in this family does it mean I will be the first or last to die? Or will it be Jack because, well, he just came here, didn't he?"

"I'm sure it won't be Jack," Mum said with a melty smile. "Peanut, why must you insist upon talking about death?"

"Oh . . . only when I think about it, Mum. And me and Jack *were* in Korea . . . and there was a lot of dyin' goin' on."

"I understand."

"Why do you always smile like that when you say, 'I understand'?"

"Do I? I was thinking of something Mrs. Allsop said and I was really feeling sad."

"Tell us, Mum."

"Oh, it was nothing . . . well . . . if you must know. Then you have to go to sleep," Mum said in that chicky little way like a mother hen. "Mrs. Allsop said, 'I'm glad Duck's too young for Korea, Nance. It's hard enough to get through life at home these days: what with tablets to slow ya heart down and clocks inside you to keep them ticking; cars goin' faster and kids with money to buy 'em. Seems the old are dyin' older and the young are dyin' younger . . . and us in between, in our prime and glory, have to foot the bills!' "

"Gee, and I *am* young, Mum. Does she mean I'll die before Granfarver Jones?"

"I didn't mean that! Peanut, you've got to promise me you'll stop thinking about death. You'll become an . . . Invetera Hypochon . . ."

If you think I'm even going to try and remember those words you're sillier than Cinderella for wearing glass shoes.

"I'll try, Mum . . . but I can't promise."

"That's all I ask for now," Mum said, and patted the bedclothes around me, even though they were very very tidy. It must have been a very tidy nightmare. "Now get some shuteye." That's a Dad good night.

I pretended to go to sleep. What I was really thinking was that if I got a slow bike instead of a fast car I'd live longer than Granfarver Jones any-bloody-how. And that wasn't thinking about dying, was it? Maybe it *was* something to do with death, but it was thinking about not dying, the way I figured it . . . unless I was Granfarver Jones, which I'm not . . . thank God for Sundee-in-Harlem.

"That old sonofabitch was around before the Seventh Day," Dad said.

9

"TELL ABOUT IT AGAIN, Granfarver. Tell about why the people stopped chiselling the big stump to bits and turned it into a bench instead."

"Oh, no!"

"For Chrissake let the dicey old bastard get it over with. You can't put it off any longer."

"Well . . . I wasn't much more than a nipper at the time . . ."

"Last time he told it he was married to Granma Jones and she was working beside him when *it* happened."

"It was Sunday mornin'. Me an' Bill Marchant was chisellin' away. I remember him because he borrowed a bob for a few beers and never paid me back."

"Wonder what the brew was like in them days?"

"There was Addle'eaded 'Arry Adlington. Mike Feegan . . . oh, and old Jack Kerr: he woulda been your great-great-great-grandad, Peterdan."

"Hear that, Chooky? Whatya think about that?" Peterdunny said.

"I think you're gonna be a blabbermouth like Granfarver," Chooky said.

"I heard that, son! Then there was Ted 'Oward who took the government surveyors through the Pass because Oxford was busy explorin' up the Darlin' by that time."

"My mother's sorta related to him," Connie said.

"Bull . . . you wanna be in everything except a dress, Connie. Whatya doin' here, anyhow? This is a boys' gang."

"I'm stayin'," Connie said. "You can put your fists where your lip is if you're game."

"Quit squawkin' an' listen," Granfarver said. "We was all hackin' away when it happened, and it put everything and everbody outa kilter. It musta been about lunch time because, I just remember, Minnie Kerr and young Annie Howard had come over with some tucker for us. Now, it wasn't the sun because the sun was already over the lake. This came from across Ol' Man Kaiser, but it was just called the Skull then . . ."

"Gee, the Skull! Wish it was still called the Skull, don't you, Chooky?"

". . . before the German climbed it and called it after the Kaiser. Now this thing shined up into the sky, but not yellow like sunlight. It wasn't any rainbow because it was straight up and down and was whitey lookin'. It started movin' towards Boomeroo like a Godamighty walking stick of light . . . with the hiccoughs . . . in hoppity-skippity movements."

"Hiccups, Granfarver."

"Strufe . . . weren't you frightened, Granfarver?"

"Nooh. But Annie and Minnie got scared."

"They was women, that's why!"

"And they sorta clung to me in little huggy ways."

"Why di'n't Minnie Kerr cling to my great-great-great-grandad insteada clingin' to you?"

"Because she was 'is sister; and because they was both stuck on me."

"Gee, Granfarver. I woulda run away from it!"

"We all know that, Peterdunny. You'd run away from chickenshit if it was still hot."

"It kept comin' closer and comin' closer, like a bloody big topless tree holding up heaven. Or maybe it was more like as if heaven had a hole in it and this grand shinin' light was suckin' up the valley in a big funnel. *Then it stopped*. Right over the half-chiselled stump. Then magiclike . . . I'll bet my last razoo on this . . . it melted onto the top of that bloody ugly old root and run down the chiselled sides all veinlike . . . shivery and shiny in silver ripples. Sorta lookin' like a tickle feels."

"The old cunt's getting poetic."

Here Granfarver Jones always trembles and little waterfalls of emotion cause him to jitter, his chin gibbering noiselessly.

There is no doubt that whatever affected him those many years before, on the spot where the Death Seat now stands, still has the power to entrance him in a mild terror. His whole fat but faggot-boned body creates a congeries of horror. The kids swallow it whole as if they were watching Dracula and the Bride of Frankenstein mate.

"Jings, Granfarver . . . go on!"

"It just soaked into the bloody ground!" Granfarver said. "Then Addle'eaded 'Arry went over and touched it."

"Was he brave!"

"No, just stupid as a Chadla chook. He rubbed his hand on it then licked his fingers and grinned and . . ."

"Dropped dead, Granfarver?"

". . . gave us that bloody big bucktooth grin a second time an' said, 'It's water.' "

Granfarver always spat at this stage. Never failed to.

Usually a bilious beauty, and if he happened to be telling the story in his own back yard some nearby scratching hen would pounce on it. All the Jones's chickens were partial to tobacco juice.

"Then Minnie Kerr, who went into a trance next day and never came out till the turn of the century, started moaning: 'It's an omen. It's an omen. It's the end of the world comin'.' Annie 'Oward slapped her face good and hard. There's some say it was the slap put her in the trance. But Minnie was silly as a wet hen and wouldn've known an omen from a 'omin' pigeon."

Granfarver piled that joke into whatever version he told. You could roll your own on it.

"Course, Annie 'Oward was just waitin' for a chance to bash Minnie anyhow because she was jealous of the way Minnie always cottoned onto me."

"I don't fink *that* Minnie Kerr was related to my great-great-great-grandad," Peterdunny said.

"Sure she was, ya drongo!" Chooky said. "Hey . . . hear that . . . Peterdunny comes from a long line of loonies."

"Shut your floggin' mouth," Peterdunny said.

A woman's voice from inside the house invaded the storytelling world: "I can hear you children out there!"

"The women in your house's got great floppin' ears, Granfarver. How can you bear it?"

"If I said it was easy, son, it'd be like sayin' piss was as good as beer. I'd rather live without 'em and drink piss all me life than have to put up with 'em and have the beer laid on forever."

"What about Addle'eaded 'Arry, Granfarver?"

"Er? Oh . . . that fool. He was fulla shi . . . ock," Granfarver said, his interest shucked. "We took him to the ambulance tent, him and Minnie. Him sayin' it was only water! How would he know? Only ever tasted water once in his life, the time he nearly drowned in the creek. We knew it wasn't . . . not even rain water, because rain don't come along in a sorta private spout . . ."

"I can hear me mum screeching, Granfarver. Gotta go! *You* comin', Chooky?"

"Yeah. You better scoot, too, Peterdunny."

"Fanks, Granfarver. 'Ooray, Connie!"

" 'Ooroo, Granfarver."

The old man was no longer with them: the simmering sunlight and the soft simpering of the foraging hens around his rocking chair had already manoeuvred him into another world. A few complaining crows flew over and ah-ahed down at the departing kids.

Whatever it had been that had imprinted itself upon Granfarver Jones's shuttered memories made people change their minds about the mighty old stump.

The war was over. The hate gone. They chiselled now with plans and compassion. Peace and love turned them into creators and the warmth butterflied into ambition. Their transformed hearts inspired their hands. The sun shone but the world was shadowless. Maybe it *had* been an omen. They were able to see what wasn't there, these townspeople who became artisans, their fingers like blessed tools anointing what was left of the tree trunk. As the work progressed and they realized that the half which remained could be fashioned into an enormous pew, the sheer joy of it gathered force and bound them in an immensity of happiness.

"Let's make it a monument."

"We could design a garden around it."

"A playground?"

"We should send to Italy for a sculptor to finish it off properly."

"Oh, leave the fuckin' thing like it is."

What luck! Common sense prevailed and there was no titivating it. Main Road and Cambridge Street were cut back at their four married corners to give traffic a roundabout space.

Its reputation to calm a hot hand and a dizzy head spread. There was no official unveiling, just a late, last shift gathering at the corner shanty.

"I reckon the bloody thing's as finished as it'll ever be. You could slip up and down it all night, naked as an Abo on walkabout and never get a splinter in yer arse."

"We oughta go back over there and christen it, but . . . unofficially."

"Piss on it?"

"That's what I mean."

"Line up!"

"Did your piss ever look so pure?"

"That's the moonlight caught in the piss twist."

There it was and there it remained, piss-launched and weather-worthy. The Death Seat. A semicircular, high-backed, high-shouldered bench. A community seat. Beautiful in its austerity. Gracious in strength. Classic beyond the get of the civilization that produced it. True to its deep enduring nature. Practical in that it belonged to where it was. If that isn't art then only death is.

10

MIND YOU, we don't remember much before Jack Rivers came. I told you he was a perfect little gentleman, didn't I? Not cheeky. His feet are never dirty and his face always clean . . . and his outlook bright; Mum said so. Dad would say he didn't tub much, but then he never gets messy. And even though I sometimes have a sip of Mum or Dad's beer, Jack's lips are . . .

"Untouched by demon rum," Mum said.

"How abart that?" Dad said.

"Don't stop him from having a big mouth," Connie said. "You name it and Roamin' Rivers either did it before, invented it . . . or blew it."

"My goodness, Peanut," Mum said in that pretty surprised voice when she doesn't want to listen to what Connie's fiddly-doodling on about, "how do you get so dirty? Look at Johnnie, as clean as the moment he went outside to play. He shan't need a bath tonight."

"What's this shan't?" Dad said. "Like an engine shunts?"

Jack is better looking than Jerry Kyle, but Connie says

Swiftie Madison would leave him for dead. The laundrette ladies talk a lot about Jerry but not much about Swiftie because they all love him, and it seems they have more fun saying things that are not nice about people.

"If Jerry Kyle was a girl, Flo, he'd be prettier than Goldie Killorn . . . but what if he was . . . well, like his mother?"

"Goldie Killorn was ugly as a child. Remember?"

And can they remember? These women have memories like swallows . . . that come back more often.

"Pretty kids go off and ugly ones come on, Zelda," Mrs. Allsop said. "My boy, Duck, will grow into a handsome man. A swan of a man!"

"But soon as men reach their prime they go off almost the next day. Not like us women. We have years in our prime and glory."

"Where I am right now, Esmay. Yes, men have a prime and I suppose a few of them have a moment of glory but they're never in their prime *and* glory like a woman who's sorta matured gradually, so to speak."

"Goldie was never gradual. She bloomed overnight."

"And Ben Leslie plucked 'er."

"She really getting married this time?"

"To a photographer?"

"He took her picture in the nude for a snooty magazine; but there's a white bar with advertisements on it across the . . . vital spots."

"Ben Leslie's been behind *that* bar!"

"Esmeralda Ackerson saw the weddin' in Mrs. Killorn's teacup. And Esmeralda ain't been wrong since Rivette won the Melbourne Cup."

"Anybody 'eard what Ben Leslie's got to say?"

"Heard? In this town? Want me to tell you how many times your old man went home drunk last week, Mattie?"

* * *

Goldie and Ben did have a chance to have coffee.

"Why marry him? Live with him. You've always been a stickler for equality."

"For as short a time as you hope, Ben?"

"It won't last."

"You're so damned positive."

"And you so volatile."

"As you paint me. Now, Ben, you must take this watch back. Now and . . . *here*."

"Is he that old-fashioned?"

"Yes."

"Love!" Ben said. "It's like anything else you think you want. Your imagination has to buy it first . . . but by then the best is over."

"For someone like you who *can* buy anything."

"I don't understand this you."

"You don't understand what it's like to be an Australian woman, that's why, Ben."

"God, I hope never."

"Darcy understands a woman. In some ways he's . . ."

"Bi?"

"You know me better than that . . . and you will not rile me."

Those laundrette ladies know everything about everybody . . . except Jack Rivers. Jack is too clever for them, and can do anything he sets his mind to.

"Maybe," Connie said, "but there's lotsa things unset about him. Like one of Mum's junkets . . . and they make vomit look good. He's a weak reed, that's what Mr. Riverina is."

"Jack isn't weak on anything, thank you very much and mind your own business, Connie."

" 'Cept the stomach," Connie said.

"I heard that, Connie," Mum said. "You'll be sorry when

The Boys have grown up and all they have is memories of you nagging them."

"And her big ears," Connie whispered, and then said aloud, "I wish they'd both go on walkabout."

"Jack Rivers flew an aeroplane once. Did you know that, Connie?"

"He couldn't fly an Aeroplane Jelly to the bottom of the bowl," Connie said, and laughed like a maddy. "Bert Hinkler he isn't."

She called him Jack Hinkler for a few days. Then Smithie Rivers. Then Lindy Riverbergh. Then something that sounded like Shark Mermoz . . . I don't know why except Connie knows a lot about Early Flyers. She usually brings them up when she's feeling doomed.

"Doomed! Doomed!" Connie wails. "All us Early Flyers are doomed. Hinkler's gone. Smithie's gone. Amelia's gone. Mermoz's gone. There's only me . . . and maybe Lindy."

"For a doomed man Lindbergh's livin' a long life," Dad says.

Then they have this Regular Argument about whether Lindy is alive, gone or still doomed. Mum and Jack and me prefer it when they have their Cut-and-dried Arguments, take a few pokes at each other and get it over with . . . and off the menu, as Mum says.

Jack Rivers drove the roaringest Express of all, once.

"Clear the track!" Connie shouted. "Here comes Casey Rivers, the railway dingbat, striking out."

And once (I wish I had done this) he steered the Kincomba picnic ferryboat all the way to Inch Island and then right across Lake MacDonald to Boolawoy, where the waves are frothier than the foam in Mum's bubble bath.

"And people who weren't seasick were riversick," Connie said, laughing to fill a boot.

She was so mean I didn't tell her about the day (she was

at school) Dad got into a foamy tub with Mum and had
fun. Jack and me listened to the joking and splashing and
oohing and aahing. They sure had more fun than when
Mum gives us a bath.

"Here comes the real foam," Dad said, like as if he was
going to a fire and the ladder went up before he got the
engine there. "Or should I say the foamy come?"

"Tony . . . shhhh," we heard Mum whisper.

"Are you comin', honey?"

"I think so, but keep it low."

"God, it's higher than it's been for years!"

We had no idea where they were going to or coming
from with all that sudsy stuff over them; and we didn't
hear Mum answer if she did come or go or went with him
. . . wherever you can go in a tub because they never left
the bathroom.

"Jack Rivers this, Jack Rivers that," Connie said. "I swear
to God I wish that kid had never set foot in this house. He
oughta be in a geometry book, that's where, he's so damn
square."

"Jack's a good boy!" I said.

"Dad thinks he's a dingaling," Connie said.

"*Liar!*" I shouted. I did, too.

"You're a sonofabitch when you want to be, Connie,"
Dad said, almost furious for once. "By whose standards do
you set yourself up? Let him be! Honestly, I don't think
you're mine. Some bloody Fuller Brush Man musta called
when I was in the Islands."

"To the best of my knowledge there's never been a Fuller
Brush Man in this town," Mum said.

"Your knowledge is not always enough, Nance."

"Oh, go jump in a . . . wake," Mum said.

"Sometimes I hate that Yank," Connie said to me and
Jack once.

"Poor Dad . . . he's your buddy, too."

"That's nothing," she said, like an elephant thwacking a fly. "Sometimes I get so steamed up I could hate God . . . if I knew where I could get my hands on Him. Bet that shakes the britches off Chicken Jack!"

"But, Connie . . . that's . . ."

"I can't think of a word for it either," Connie said. "Just wanted to let you know how mad I could get. So thank your lucky tin stars I don't come riding through that must-be town of yours on Rocky Ned, the greatest outlaw horse of them all. We'd rip yous apart, all the way from Frisco to St. Jo."

"Connie, I heard that!"

"Just rehearsin' some American talk for when we visit our relatives," Connie said in her smartest-arse way.

"*Yous* is neither American nor English," Mum said, coming to the bedroom door in one of her snippetty moods — when she doesn't even speak to me or Jack.

"Must be Australian, well," Connie said.

"You're getting just too much of a damn flibbertigibbet." She went away like a black cloud looking for a storm, muttering, "I'm only human after all."

"That new German kid calls his mum, Mutta," Connie said. "It figures!"

Mum doesn't get her I'm-only-human mood very often; and we're glad she doesn't get human like this too much, much as we love her.

Connie frowned and said, "The Monthlies. Big Myrt gets them already . . . hope I never do. You Two better keep outa my way, too, for the rest of the day."

"We will." We were really praying that Connie never ever did get those Monthlies: she's mean enough without them . . . whatever they are.

"You don't hate Jack because he's like God and you can't get your hands on him, do you, Connie?"

"I don't hate him as much as you, you crumb."

"Oh, Connie, you do love Jack!"

"Don't *hug* me. You know I don't go for that lovely-dovey crap. Now scoot! I'm gonna make meself a new pair of wings. A pair of super wings, you hear?"

She will too. I don't know what I would have done if Jack Rivers hadn't come to live with us. Things were not only crook in Muswellbrook Before Jack, but were duller than Nulla Nulla.

"I've heard more about Before and After Jack in this house than I ever heard about Before Christ when I was a kid going to chapel," Dad said.

"And that was Before Moses, wasn't it, Dad?" Connie said.

"You're being cheeky to Dad, Connie," I said.

Connie pinched my chin sneakily and whispered, "Kitchie-kitchie-koo to you too, you dirty little sonofabitch; why don't you go poo?"

Well, I guess you have to know sometime . . . or else you'll hear it from someone else: Connie does this to me to remind me that she remembers my First Perdicament better than I do.

One day when I was still a highchair baby, it seems Connie saw me looking like I used to look when I had just done what I had just done, and she dobbed me in.

"Oh-ho! Peanut's got troubles again, Mum."

Nance knew Peanut had dirtied his nappy but would have preferred to let it go till after Tony went downstairs to work as soon as breakfast was over. Then she would have given Peanut the Potty Lecture.

"Tell Mumma when you feel like it, darling."

Great! But Peanut didn't know when he felt like it; one minute he was clean and the next minute he was smelly. It was a predicament.

Tony leant across the table and slapped the little boy and Nance said, "Don't do that, Tony. You'll give him a complex."

"He's a dirty little sonofabitch," Tony said, "and I thought I told you to get him outa diapers."

"Oh, my Lord-and-Master is it this morning?" Nance said, thought twice and purred. "Give him a chance, honey. Connie went through this stage when you were in the Islands."

Islands was the magic word. "Sorry," Tony said. "He is a cute little basstid. Nobody could say I didn't knock him outa you." He pinched his son's chin softly and said, "Hi, Bub. Kitchie-kitchie-koo." The baby smiled in return because his mother didn't bark like a doggie when his father said that. "But you will try and get him out of those damn diapers, eh?"

Connie snarled quietly at Peanut behind their parents' back when Tony kitchie-kitchie-kooed the kid again.

Nance cleared the table and Tony hung round while she changed Peanut. He flipped the boy's dickie and said, "Not bad. Takes after his old man."

Connie rumbled like a thundercloud. She could change quicker than the electric light.

"Tony," Nance said and slapped him softly.

Connie gave the baby her pins-and-needles look: her tiger eyes and frown combined. It felt like nighttime behind the little fellow's eyes.

"Why can't the sun always be shining, Connie?"

"Because it would melt all the ice cream in the world, dummy," Connie said. "No . . . I'm only teasing. But I have thought about it . . . and I think I agree with God."

"You talking to God again?"

"We ain't enemies," Connie said. "I figure it this way. If

we didn't sleep and wanted the sun all the time then God would have to make another sun so the people on the other side of the world could have one. See?"

"You are smart, Connie."

"And everyone knows one is cheaper than two. And for all we know God might be on a budget like Mum is. Only I bet he ain't complaining about it all the time like That Woman."

"It's like as if the world goes away when night comes. Me and Jack always wonder if it's going to come back again. It's a bit like dying, I guess."

"You silly boy, it's not a bit like dying," Connie said. "And I thought Mum told you to forget about dying. You'll get like old Jeannie Moir. Every week she's dying . . . but she's the only person I heard of ever getting over Galloping Consumption."

We were just too taken back to ask about that one. What a lovely sound! *Galloping Consumption.* That's the way I want to die. Bravely, of course. I'll ask Monte Howard about it because he's an expert on cowboy pictures. That must be the way the Goodies go. Because all the Baddies die in the gun fight. We just owaaaad at Connie that time.

"I have this lousy feeling you're going to be in my hair all my life," Connie said.

"You can be nice, Connie. You make me feel good saying I'll live as long as you, even though I know I'll die."

"Of course you will, twit . . . eventually."

"I said you was nice."

"Grandma Leo says creaking doors never fall. So don't worry, Peanut. Besides, you'll only be in the dark for another year or so. I remember when I was seven. It was like someone switched on a dirty big light and I suddenly saw all that was going on around me. Gosh, it was super!"

Connie's not much of a gosher.

"The things that suddenly hit me in the eye. Like how yukkie boys are . . . and what money's really for: *to save and feel rich*. And how it's better havin' people begging you for something instead of being a scrounger yourself. Like having power. Being able to swim without being scared of sharks. Not bein' scared of spiders. Knowing why it's dark . . . because the sun's round the other side of the world so the Yanks can sunbake, too. Wait till you see the light, buster. If you've got any sense you'll be like me and get some *power*."

If money's not for lollies and ice cream I don't want to know. I swear to you Connie's never spent a penny since she started school. She never waited to be seven for that part of her power. When she was five Mum said she had a party and sold all her birthday presents back to the kids that brought them for half price . . . or whatever the kids had in their pockets at the time. I bet by now her stool is heavier than the bricks she's got on top of it. Me and Jack and Mum (secretly) call her the Bricklayer. Duck Allsop couldn't even lift her money box let alone sneak it into his mother's laundry bag. When I come to think of it, but, she's still not a bad scrounger herself; either that or she's a better thief than Duck Allsop. She's at her best when she's doing her homework.

"Tell Kid Rivers to come here," Connie said. "Even a know-all like him can always learn a little more from these homework books of mine."

"Gee, Connie, it must be good and powerful just to be able to use a pen instead of a pencil."

"It comes with the light," Connie said, cutting short my crap. "See this sum: it's called long division. I'm a whizz at arithmetic. Not so crash-hot at sewing, but I can put numbers through a loop. Geography and history so-so, but arithmetic . . . I think I'll be a bank manager when I grow up."

That was about the first and last time I ever heard Connie talk about being grown up.

"Dad's good at jography," I said.

"That's jogging! Geography teaches you all this lousy stuff about everywhere in the world except where you live. Don't expect to find Boomeroo in your school atlas. We might as well be livin' in Woop Woop."

"Well, wasn't Jack Rivers lucky to find it?"

"There's a lotta doubt about how good or lucky that day was. Wanna hear what I'm learning for the school concert this year?"

"Oh, Connie, are you going to be in the concert this year, too, and be ... magnificent again, and ... ?"

"Don't get blown away! I'm not a star yet. The boys hog all the best parts," Connie said. "Now me and Maggie and Big Myrt are swaggies and come on humpin' our blueys, and wearing old hats with fly-corks swinging round the edge. And we're wearin' bowyangs . . . that's like when you tie rope round the legs of your pants to stop snakes from crawling up. The boys call them shit catchers . . . and that's why they wouldn't be in this part of the concert."

"That's rude."

"It's a rude world, Peanut. You can't live in this little laundry dump all your life. Now, are you gonna listen or you wanna make a call on the minister about rude things."

"We're listenin'!"

"Maggie says: 'Let's camp by this billabong, mates.' And Big Myrt says: 'We'll build a fire and boil the billy, ready for a singsong when the shearers get here.' There's a bit more corny stuff while we're waiting for the shearers to come and sing 'The Banks of the Condamine,' then I step forward and recite:

Though poor and in trouble I wander alone,
With a rebel cockade in my hat;

Though friends may desert me, and kindred disown,
My country will never do that!
You may sing of the shamrock, the thistle, the rose,
Or the three in a bunch, if you will;
But I know of a country that gathered all those,
And I love the great land where the waratah grows,
And the wattle-bough blooms on the hill."

"That was wonderful, Connie . . . wasn't it wonderful, Jack?"

"Aw, I can improve on that. I'm gonna get up there and be meself."

"And you can be yourself better than anyone we know. What's a rebel cockade, Connie?"

"A thing battlers wear in their hats to show they're game. Like a feather."

"Jack Rivers is as game as they come," I said.

"Guess that's why all those bushrangers who died game . . . went," Connie said.

Isn't she quick? I hate her when she don't give me a chance to be clever.

"Did all the bushrangers die?"

"Peanut! Everybody dies! Show me someone, anyone, and I'll tell you someone who's gonna die some day. Now lay off. Get lost! Go die if you want, but forget it."

One day, years earlier, after getting such a brush-off from Connie, Peanut wandered into the front part of the shop where all the skinny, fat and rude women came to disperse flapdoodle while the Bendix machines did their wash. He went in quietly and rested behind one of the soap-sloshing monsters . . . and all he did was unscrew one little reddy sort of thumb at the back. Suddenly that particular monster shuddered and spat sparks at him. Flicketty-flack-flack-

flack. He was brave and tried to catch some of the cracker sparks but they bit him, so he raced round to the front of that terrible machine shaking his fingers. It felt as if a million bully ants had bitten him. Now all the machines started to burra-burra, and the swimming clothes were flipping and flopping backwards and forwards instead of spinning. Then they began to slow down as if they were going to grab him to swish him round. The bubbly noises stopped altogether and the machines all died. Peanut felt funny and fell down as if he was zapping off to sleep or maybe dying himself.

One of the skinny-assed trollops screeched: "Mr. Delarue! Mr. Delarue! Your little boy . . . he's been *Eleckerkuted*."

A fat young sheila cried out in anguish, as well as she could with a mouthful of jelly beans. "Oh, poor little Peanut . . . is he dead?" This was Feet-feet Anderson. She was a nice, overfed whore, and often gave Peanut and Jack some of her everlasting lollies.

"All fat sheilas can eat!" Connie said. "Gawd, can Big Myrtle chomp. She'd eat Ajax and chase Billy Cook."

Mrs. Allsop kept talking all through the crisis.

"She's a yakkaholic," Dad said. "Talk herself to death on the thought of the Sydney phone book."

Tony rushed in and picked up the melted little eleckerkuted heap. Swooshed it up into his big strong arms and hugged it tight.

"Bub? Are you OK? Bub?" He put his hand inside the little shirt and felt a wildly beating heart in a tiny body come to life busting for joy to find itself so safe and sound in those father arms.

Peanut opened his eyes and saw two big tears in his dad's eyes, shining the way street lamps do on a wet night. Christmas-candly.

"All he does now is give me and Jack Rivers the Big-eye when he's angry. There are no tears in the Big-eyes, I can tell you that."

When Connie says, "Dad's giving You Guys the Big-eye," The Boys smile and pretend maybe the iron cord somehow got stuck to their fingers.

After hugging Peanut, Tony took him to the back of the shop. When he realized the only shock his son was suffering from was the laundrette ladies' screaming shit he put the kid down and said, "Sit tight, Junior." Then he yelled upstairs: "Hey, Nance. How's about keeping your baby outa my shop?"

As soon as Tony left and Peanut was alone sitting-tight-Junior, with his head in his hands and sucking his lips, *he* arrived. Just like that. They were the best of friends right from the very start. Jack Rivers . . . a boy for all reasons.

"My Jack!"

Later, when Peanut tried to explain it to Connie, she said, "The way you sit, sucking your lips over your teeth like a chimp, it's a wonder Tarzan or Cheetah didn't come and sit beside you instead of another little drongo."

Peanut scurried upstairs to tell his mother.

"What's Dad so crabby about? If you came up for a romp on the beds you're too late, darling; they're already made up."

"Mum, I got a liddel fren come to play. Can 'e stay for lunch?"

"Of course," Nance said. "I'm glad. I thought you were going to be a loner all your little life. Tell him to come in and park his little bottom at the table. First in best fed. Connie will be home soon."

"He's name's Jack Rivers, Mum."

"His name," Nance said. "That's a lovely name. They must be new in town. You and Jack sit there. Daddy will be up any minute like a bull at a picnic . . . and a tale longer than a tiger's . . . so don't get under his feet. Where is . . . Jack?"

"Sittin' right here next to me, Mummy."

"Oh . . . oh . . . of course. I must be going blind." Nance moved Jack's plate, which she had set in the middle of one side, closer to Peanut.

Tony came up, washed his hands, then looked at the extra plate. "We got company?"

"Yes, honey," Nance said, and pretended to stick the bread knife into Tony's belly. "A little friend of Peanut's, come to lunch."

Nobody knew at this stage that Jack had come to stay.

"Where the hell is he?" Tony said.

Nance nudged him again with the bread knife and whispered to him. "Right there next to Peanut," she said aloud.

"*Ohhhhhhhh.*" Tony gave a silly gush then a sillier sigh as he sat down. He gave Peanut an unloving look. "How abart that?"

"His name is Jack Rivers, Dad."

"Sure. Well, you keep him and yourself outa the laundry this afternoon and we'll get on fine." Tony hunched his big Father Bear shoulders, then spread his arms as he did when he was going to take a belly flopper in the lake just to make the kids laugh. Peanut thought he was going to say: Who's been eating my lunch? But he said, "Don't let it throw you, Bub. With me it's white snakes."

Connie came home for lunch as though the school bell would ring before her first gulp. She kept looking at Jack Rivers's plate, then at Peanut and then at Tony and Nance. The way birds check everything before they make their splash into a fountain. She was building up a big silence out of nothing-blocks. Finally she put her fork down —

Connie ate like her father — folded her arms and said, "Hasn't someone got news for me?"

Tony roared and said, "He's a friend of Fella's, Connie, and his name's Jack Rivers."

"Oh, my aching heart, what a name," Connie said and then she roared like Tony.

Nance put a stop to their private woolsoomooloo.

"I've got news for you, Young Lady. You've got to go to the store for me before you go back to school, so burn it up."

"Oh, Mum, do I gotta?"

"You have to ... if that's what you mean."

So Jack Rivers came and Jack Rivers stayed. Dad and Connie laughed at him a lot at first and used to call him the Funniest Little Guy Imaginable. They would go into fits and me and Mum and Jack despaired for them at times.

"I mean to say, Dad," Connie said, "you can't say anything else, can you ... except *unimaginable?*" And off they'd go again into giggleland.

But Jack and me got used to it and, after all, Mum loved Jackie from the very beginning. And when it's Show-poker Time in our house I'd rather have Mum on my side than Big Myrtle Worthington even.

Dad knows this, too, because once we heard him say to Mum, "Maybe you are the Great Big Pig at Show-poker Time, but when it's Show-peter Time in bed they don't come any bigger than me."

We don't know anything about Show-peter Time but maybe it's something Yanks are big at like whopping off. I s'pose I'll have to learn about it, but, because I am a little bit Yank.

"He's sexy like me," Dad said. "Break as many hearts, too, I bet."

"Let's hope he's not as lippy about it as you," Mum said.

Jack and me are more smiley than lippy.

"Go on," Connie said once when we were in Deep Trouble (and trouble don't come any troubler than Deep Trouble in Delarueland), "let's see you smile your way out of this an' I'll personally pay for your funeral, you little deadbeat."

See, I told you Connie could be nice.

"What if nobody wants to give you a funeral, Connie?"

"They throw you on the rubbish heap with the rest of the garbage. What did you think, dimwit? Someone was going to wrap you up in brown paper and post you to heaven?"

"That's a pretty good idea," I said. Jack and me slept on that for a few nights and couldn't come up with anything better. You can't beat Connie even when she's not trying to win. She'll probably bamboozle St. Peter when she gets to the Pearly Gates.

"Your friends bury you if you leave money," Dad said. "And your enemies get together and do it when you start to stink if you die broke."

"Antony!"

I don't have to tell you who that was.

We liked Connie's idea better so when I'm ten and have a bike I'm going to ride down to the big post office at Kincomba and fix it up with them to post me straight to heaven when I die. I'll just have to make sure I have enough brown paper and string hidden to wrap me in, because if I leave it layin' around Connie will steal it and make another kite with it . . . and I'd be *left* to stink because I won't have enough money left for my friends to bury me. I'll probably have spent it all on lollies and ice cream as fast as I get it . . . like I do now. And I haven't got any enemies . . . I don't think . . . that's a Real Perdicament. I might have to . . . browse on it.

On the other hand there's always Jack Rivers: he'll come

up with something else, sometime, I'm sure. Jack's the boy in a pinch.

That doesn't mean Jack's a thief . . . but I guess you know what it means. It's a Mum saying.

"There'll be nothing of Jack to bury," Connie said. "That's one problem the Great River doesn't have to worry about."

"Connie, watch it," Mum said. "You go too far."

"I just meant Jack might starve to death if you don't feed him more, Mum," Connie said. God, she's quick!

But it's true, Jack only eats a scraping of this and a smidgen of that.

When Grandma Leo last visited she said, "Jack's got what I call a dainty appetite. He'll never have my problem." She took another slice of bread.

"Mother," Mum said. I love the way Mum says "Mother." We practise saying it that way. "Let's face it. Your problem only begins with the bread you eat; and it's not going to end with the beer you drink."

"Buy a tighter pair of corsets, Leo," Connie said, "and give me your old ones."

11

HAPPILY, Boomeroo is not precisely paradise. Unfortunately not Utopia. An enshrined Eden maybe, but not the supreme spot; for people are allowed to, and do, make mistakes and, like Eden, it has a blight. The apple in this garden is the sulphur from the Boomeroo Cement Works, the town's mainstay.

"Christ! I thought we agreed not to talk about that."

"As the grub said to his mate: 'Make like birdshit, here comes the magpie.' "

The sulphur is one of the reasons the Death Seat got its name: the main. The coal dust was minor. The Death Seat is not to be confused with the American Electric Chair.

From the outskirts of the town, the giant plant that is Boomeroo's commercial lifeline seems to sit in everybody's back yard: it is so near and enormous. Instant background. And Boomeroosters belong to that Gargantua as naturally as they belong to the Co-operative Store, as naturally as that mountainous yellow blur behind the conglomeration of steel and iron belongs to the landscape and their lives.

"*How Green Was My Valley* it ain't," Tony Delarue argued.

An east wind or a southerly, after prospecting through the valley, blows the sulphur away from Boomeroo and dusts the mountain a canary hue. A north wind, like a lunatic weather experiment, catapults itself over Mount Kaiser with such energy it has blown itself half-way to heaven before it returns to the coastal earth and scoots through Kincomba.

"It hits Kincomba like a bad breath from Mars."

"They reckon there's things livin' on Mars. Wonder if they drink beer?"

"I'd shout 'em a beer. After all, I shout cunts from Wollondonga like you."

"Some idiot from Tuggeroo saw a Flying Saucer."

"That was just the reflection of Big Fat Nellie's pussy when she was crossing the old bridge."

"Aw . . . they're edgy in Tugga lately 'cause the Kincomba Council's goin' to form a Tuggeroo Fishin' Co-op."

"Why not? They've got their dicks in every other hole in the valley."

"I think it's a good idea."

"Shut up, grub! When they put a tongue in your mouth they ruined a good arsehole."

When a westerly blows through Oxford Pass Boomeroo gets it in all the facial places where it hurts, pell-mell and suddenly. They call it the Specialist after a Kincomba eye-, nose-, and throat-specialist the local GPs refer them to when their antrum problems get past the aspirin stage.

This whipping wind traces a weird choreography upon the sulphur breasts, then lashes through the auditorium of the town, a dancing cohort of rubbish caught in its pollen punches. It can deform a day quicker than a flood warning, wreck a weekend or spoil whole consecutive week days. Like unseen flames, its long arms, buttressing its bastardy, can suffocate a house.

The westerly rides in from the combustible heart of the Outback and, like the hobo it is, has no feeling for any place. It can enlist a compost heap and make it a frightening force. Entice a loose shutter to drive a woman crazy. Encourage trees to battle and moan and scare the wits and shit out of kids at night. Turn a street into a channel of malice. Add dangers to corners, weight to loads, temperament to character, and excuses to lies. No clown or showoff like the Southerly Buster and willy-willy, it has persistent tricks. It can chase a sheet of corrugated iron for miles in hops, skips and jumps; mow a riderless pushbike across several lawns and gardens. It can pile Lake MacDonald across to Boolawoy and have the Boolawoysters wondering which side of their sand dunes is the ocean. Swipe your hat across somebody else's face. Drop a Boomeroo chicken in a Chadla back yard. Kids can lean against it without any fear of falling on their faces.

When it has a natural ally like the hill-high sulphur pile it makes the most of it and gives Boomeroo a big unrationed gutful.

"In the olden days, Coral, doctors used to give you a spider dipped in sulphur and honey for a cure-all."

Yet, in spite of all this violence from the westerly, it is not as aggravating as the infiltrating sulphur smell itself, which is always there. The presence of it can blemish a balmy night when there isn't even a hiss of a breeze in the entire valley. This they hate. This seeping. They cough and curse it.

A few, like Granfarver Jones, insist that the sulphur is beneficial. "I've never minded it," the old bastard said. "The sulphur never killed anybody off. Look at me! I've been coal-dusted as well. When I was young we used to take Epsom salts on a sixpence for a headache; and sulphur on a shilling for a pain in the gut."

"He's the only bloody real pain left in the town now."

They lived with it because it was part of the body of their lives. Those who worked in the sulphur shed did so as a matter and manner of survival, whether or not it extended or shortened their existence.

"I wouldn't work in the sulphur-fuckin'-shed if they paid me by the suckin' second."

"You wouldn't work if you was a fuckin' ant, you lazy fuckin' grub."

Not so long before, the men did not retire at sixty or sixty-five but worked until they were seventy or over, or until only God knew their age . . .

"What people don't realize these days is that work keeps ya alive."

. . . and those that worked in the sulphur shed were presumably doomed — if dying at eighty could be called doom. They collected at the Death Seat, a happy group through the years, after they had quit their lifetime of work. They sat through the springs and summers and autumns on that big bench in the middle of Boomeroo, knowing that sometime during the coming winter one or two of them would die.

Not even the westerly could disturb their dozing memories or their yarning, because the Death Seat had its broad, time-upholstered back to Oxford Pass.

Facts did not worry them, and they were not interested in new-fangled drugs or old-fangled miracles. Their pensions were not embracing enough, but they doubted if their lives needed compensating. You can't compensate something that has been filled. Their ilk has gone. You know it and I know it and the world knows it. They knew where they were going, and we do not; and all we can do is shed tears that our analysing natures have stripped us of everything they were trying to leave us.

For the most part their lives had been composed of simply knowing how to live together; and their only secret had been steady work.

"They reckon they're puttin' in one of them bundy clocks."

"You mean they're gonna time men the way they clock greyhounds and horses?"

"That won't work! How long you're at the plant's got nothing to do with how hard you work."

They believed in functional smoking.

"They got septic tanks at work now, and you can't flush any rubbish down . . . how come?"

"Kills the maggots in the tank or somethin'."

"Gawd . . . shut up, it's nelly tucker-time."

"What worries the young fellas most is you can't throw ya butts in the septic."

"An' you're only supposed to have two ciggies a day . . . at smoko."

"Hell! Why else go for six shits a day if you can't flush ya butts?"

They were not so old they didn't remember their sex lives.

"You'll go before me, mate; and it won't be the sulphur if you keep chatting up old Maisie Taylor. She's got more'n cancer in her pants."

"That old moll still alive?"

"The young fellas do as they're told in bed now."

"That's why they spend their nights in the pub."

"When I was young if you said you was up all night it wasn't mindin' the baby."

"You boastin' old grub. When you was young the only thing you could scrape all night was yer dinner plate."

They were for rational freedoms.

"If the miners go on strike the plant workers'll have to join 'em or else the buggers'll have all the bloody booze drunk before four o'clock."

"You reckon women *are* equal?"

"They're bloody stubborn enough."

Their excesses were limited.

"I can loan you a quid. That's all! What the hell did you do with the fifty pound you won on the bloody Cup?"

"He lost that fifty smackas at the two-up . . . di'n'ya?"

"Had a good run for me money, but. I 'ad it up to three hundred, so went to Kincomba races with Fast-arse Freddie and Sly Pork. Done the lot! Except I did give me missus five quid for squander money."

"Fast-arse Freddie made a fair living off the horses till he pulled one too many."

"Now he's so fat he couldn't even pull himself."

There was no real bitterness in these hearts and if it was the sulphur killing them they did not think it was an unfair or unkind killer. They waited without impatience or disproportionate patience. They had generally had big families, had loved and laughed, feuded and suffered, and their memories were living.

"The things they say about me when I die will probably please me but make God unhappy . . . and drive the Devil crazy."

"The nights are longer. Notice that?"

"Yeah . . . the days, too. Funny that!"

"Like as if summer and winter were getting together."

"You ever feel . . . sorry?"

"Noh! I got it all inside me. Mum, the kids, the grandchildren. Ain't as if I was goin' alone."

"Sometimes I feel sad about . . . leavin' it all."

"The sad part about it is . . . you can't . . . explain to them . . . how it is. How you've got so much to give them if they wanta listen."

"They ain't got the time."

"I read where Eskimoes put old people on ice floes."

"Like us . . . sittin' here. But we ain't cold."

When the time came they were able to say: We know you, Death. We've lived with you for a long time and seen you in different disguises. You've robbed us during wars, stolen from us in the Great Influenza Epidemic, taken our kids with diphtheria, meningitis . . . and even with lousy whooping cough. At times we beat you and dragged them back, crippled, from infantile paralysis. In fact, you seem to know us better than God at times. And we know you, Death.

We know your hand and we know your breath. And no longer have reason to be afraid of you because we know you are as much a part of life as God. You haven't been any unkinder than He has.

You must be pretty tired, too; after all, you can't look forward to the relief of death from the antics of life.

So they waited, these old men, gentled in body but unbroken in spirit: as passing a race as the Aborigines who had earlier camped beside that stump.

"I miss Old Ted."

"Never knew such skies."

"Ever hear the bloody birds so cheeky?"

"Ya know, a man could get a lot out of life if he was patient enough."

It was not necessary to say good-bye. Man and Life had been friends, and in their chemical conclusion they found Death, not the end.

Put your abacus away because no one has ever actually died upon the Death Seat, or been taken, dying, from it.

Even if their minds failed, their hearts were aware of life until the moment of truth became the moment of darkness.

"Do they still put pennies on your eyes when you die?"

12

SOME MORNINGS, if it's cold and windy and rainy, Mum brings us breakfast in bed and we stay there until she gets the Worker and the Scholar off her hands. Jack and me, we're never on her hands. Then the Home Team — We Three — have a romp on the beds. Honest. Truly. We jump up and down and have a great muck-up. Do we whoop it up? Indians on firewater and ice cream couldn't have more fun.

One morning we were lallapaloozing round more than usual and cackling like we were jackasses watching a snake charmer when Dad came hotfooting it upstairs to see what the racket was all about. He rushed in the way Connie bolts her food down at lunch time, and said in his Mr. Yankee Fixit voice, "What all's goin' on heah?"

Mum and Jack and we were all tumbled about: Mum pulled a face at Dad and said in a real cheeky-girl way, "Oh, don't be so stuffy!" As if that was something Yanks like to think they are, but aren't good at.

Dad grabbed Mum and tipped her upside down and said, "I'll stuff you! It's furburger time."

"*Antonee!*" Mum screamed. That was a new one on me. Her dress fell down over her bum and head. "Let me down this instant." Her voice was muffly.

Dad pulled the elastic in Mum's pants and it pinged. "I'd like to catapult through there right now," he said. Then he zoomed her up again and dumped her over like the ocean waves at Boolawoy tumble people. My, he is strong!

Then Mum dragged Dad down on the bed and said, "Help me pin him down, Peanut. Sit on him, Jack." She nibbled his ear and said, "We all belong to you, you poor unfortunate Yank."

"Five Little Peppers we ain't, but I want nowhere else in the world to belong, Nance," Dad said more fuzzy- than stuffy-voiced. "Let's you and me have a romp after. Haven't had furburger fer-lunch fer-ages."

Jack Rivers and me, we've *never* had furburger ever, whatever it is. Sometimes I just get tired of asking questions, so I let it go. Connie says it's . . . *Deplorable* how ignorant we are.

"You are terrible," Mum said real naughtylike. The way she says it to me and Jack if we get caught pinching a hot Betty Brown from the biscuit tray. Mum calls these oatmeal bickies Betty Browns. Isn't that a cute name for a bickie? Dad says they're Butternut Cookies from Way Back . . . which must be further back than we remember. He also calls the icing on a cake frosting, even when it's not cold. Maybe Jack and me are Deplorable. Anyway, I had this feeling Jack and me weren't going to get any furburger for lunch this day.

One afternoon when we were supposed to be having our nap we heard Mum and Dad lallapaloozing around on their big bed. Maybe that was furburger time.

"I keep forgetting how young you really are," Connie said, "till you say something as silly as that. Lallapaloozing, indeed!"

Just when Mum looked like she had decided it was fur-burger time after all, one of the fat knitty trollops sang out from downstairs in a real sweety-pie voice, "Yoo-hoo, Mr. Delarue? Mr. Delaaaarooooooohoo! I think the water's stopped running in my machine."

Mum giggled like a goosey girl.

Dad slapped her bottom and said, "I'll go down there and ram something thick and hard up her machine that'll keep the juices runnin', and her smilin', for the rest of her life." He sure sounded big and strong and full of stuff then.

Mum busted into a rambunctious fit. The bed rocked and then we all burst into bigger rambunctious fits of laughter. "We're a rum lot," Mum said.

On these mornings we can do anything except make a mess of the secret things from the Islands that Dad keeps under their bed. Gee they keep a lot of stuff under that bed. Nobody said we couldn't look. We can't imagine why they keep *pillows* there . . . under the bed! Once we got caught and Mum said, "Robin Goodfellows you are not, this morning."

We play Cowboys, Bushrangers, Spacemen and Ice Cream Men. We tchick our broom horses round, jumping from bed to bed, chasing rustlers and stopping stagecoaches.

"You must be this Baddie, Jack, and I must be the Sheriff who catches you. Then I must find out you're a Goodie-in-Disguise before Duck Allsop and the lynch mob get you."

Connie says we're still babies and she'll be glad when we're old enough to get out of the house and her hair and into the real world. Does she think we want to be cooped up here all our livelong lives?

If I try to tell her all Jack Rivers has done she says that

she doesn't think he's got much brave gravy in his gut. But when she gets too naggy and niggly . . .

"Niggardly," Mum said. She doesn't miss a trick, does she?

. . . we remind her of something I found out that upsets her.

"Connie, I discovered that Mum is older than Dad."

"So what's that got to do with the time the sun rises tomorrow?"

"Well . . . Dad *is* a lot bigger and stronger than Mum, isn't he?"

"Get to the point before you sit on it."

"Remember, it's *My Discovery*."

"Oh, fer God's sake cough it up. If it's only a brick it'll ease you."

"The way me and Jack figure is . . . when they were little Mum would've been bigger than Dad. Like you're bigger than me now." I could see her getting angry-eyed in a way that makes us happy we aren't mosquitoes on her arm. "So . . . it might just happen that some day I'll be bigger and stronger than you." Whew!

"Are you threatening me, you prawn?"

"Just looking ahead, Connie. I do intend to grow up, you know . . . like you're always telling me to."

"Well, don't let it go to your head, imbo. You might end up bein' all head and no body like Bandy-Andy."

"Even the littlest nippers are liable to shoot up like stars when they start feelin' their oats," Dad said.

"So go buy a beanstalk if you believe in fairy tales," Connie said. Damn! I had something real smart ready to say and it just bolted out of my head soon as she opened her mouth.

I'm still a bit scared to bring up My Discovery too often in case I never feel my oats and never shoot up like a star . . .

and stay a squib. But when I feel it's Absolooly Imperative to take her down a couple of pegs I remind her that the day might come when . . . you know, I'll be the big one. Bigger and taller than her.

"Than she is," Mum said.

"Connie promotes herself like she's the American eagle," Dad said.

"Or too much lion and not enough kangaroo," Mum said.

Sometimes I don't have the tiniest idea what they're talking about.

When I ask Mum about school she says I'll like it but won't say what Jack will think about it: instead she tells me things that happened to Dad when he was a little jasper at school in Ho-ho-ho . . . in Those United States.

"I'm the greatest buck ever came out of the Buckeye State," Dad said. "When I was a little jasper in Fin'lee, Oh-hi-oh, back in *the* fantabulous U-night-ted States of Am-mecca . . ."

Then it's on.

"When it's on," Mum said, "not even God or General MacArthur can turn it off."

"An' it's never been known to turn itself off," Connie said. "Seems to me General MacArthur's bigger than Ben Hall in Dad's heaven."

Then (heaven and earth forbid) he sings "Down by the Old Mill Stream," because he was born down by that old mill stream, not Down Under like us.

Sometimes Mum just ups and walks away, saying, "Fighting gamely the old onwee . . . thanks to Cole Porter." This is a kind of mumbly-sing-song saying. Not so grumbly as the Monthlies muttering. And when she's fighting-gamely-the-old-onwee she turns to Jack and me more than ever . . . we've noticed.

Jack Rivers and me have a secret secret not even Connie knows about. Some nights after Mum has put us to bed and Connie has finished her piano practice and gone to bed too ... and to sleep ...

One deep breath and Connie's dead to the world, specially the nights she has to have piano practice.

"I hate that bloody piano," Connie said. "Wish I could get some white ants. I'd teach them to play on it."

Well, if it is moonlight dark Jack and me tiptoe out onto the landing and listen to Mum and Dad downstairs. If we lie on the top step and scringe our necks we can see them sitting in their own big chairs ... or sometimes close together on the big settee. Reading or listening to the wireless and just hmm-hmming and ah-ahing each other. But sometimes they talk a lot and we look at Dad's face because he's got a lovely face at night when he's alone with Mum. Nothing like the face he wears for those fat trollops and skinny-assed females during the day. A sort of Jesus face like on my Sunday School cards. I bet my Dad has bluer eyes than Jesus, but. They shine like blue boiled lollies.

"What we gonna do about Jack when Peanut starts school?" Dad said one night.

"I really don't know. I simply don't know." Mum put her book down and looked into Daddy's lovely face. "It's not as ... bizarre as all that. Lots of children have little friends. I know people talk, but people talk about a lot of lesser things, too."

"Little friends are one thing," Dad said, "but Jack Rivers is neither little or lesser, Nance. He's a ... God Almighty ... institution! I swear he's holding up the bloody sky."

I never thought of Jack doing that, but I guess he could. That must be what an institution does.

"You should talk," Mum said. "I keep expecting his Child Endowment cheque every month."

"I would have thought he'd have moved on by now," Dad said.

"If Jack does get the wanderlust," Mum said, "you know he'll take a lot of Peanut with him."

"Hope he leaves my share," Dad said.

"Mine too," Mum said, the way she says, "Much obliged" to the ladies in the laundrette when they bring her a jar of homemade choko pickles or fig jam.

They don't always talk Jack. They go on and on some nights, but if they ever get onto the Islands, that's it. There's a lotta magic about those Islands . . . wherever they are.

"I could never ask Jack to go," Nance said. "Are you afraid to, Tony?"

"Who, *me?*" Tony said, escalating the me. "No way! Peanut and me are getting along fine lately. Last time we went for a haircut he asked me when we were goin' fishin'."

"He did?"

"Surprised, eh?" Tony said.

"Maybe we could wait until . . ."

"Jack Rivers graduates?" Tony said, and they both laughed.

"Oh, I was cleaning up today, darling, and look what I found in your old service briefcase," Nance said, producing a dried sprig of wattle.

"How abart that?"

"You always said you gave it to a Papuan girl to wear in her hair."

"The hell I did! If anyone I'd 've given it to one of the native Boys . . . they smelt better."

"I also found a poem in your handwriting."

"The very hell you did!"

"I memorized it," Nance said, with a curl in her voice

like a wriggling worm. "It's a rote little thing. *Very you.*"
She recited in a faraway tone:

> *"Do fish kiss? Eagles emote?*
> *Spiders piss? Elephants vote?*
> *Or is it we, the only beings,*
> *Who agree to all these things?"*

"Not me!" Tony said. "He was a GI who died in my arms . . . that I loved."

"Whom I loved," Nance said. "If you're trying to shock me."

"Him, I loved," Tony said.

"I'm glad . . ." Nance said, "that you kept both the poem and the wattle."

"Life plays tricks, Nance," Tony said. The melting in his eyes turned to two tears. "I don't expect you to really understand."

"I'm not a child," Nance said. "Once when I agonized whether I should go to Uni. or not, Miss Cruikshank told me: 'A person can miss a lot of education by getting too much, Nancy. You have to be a bit dispassionate to absorb years and years of education. Emotional people sometimes learn a lot more by . . . merely living.' "

"I love you, Nancy," Tony said. "Gissa kiss, as they say in Austrylia." He took one.

"Toneee!"

"All right, if you don't like French kisses . . . how about a bitta titty."

"You fool!"

"I am, I am, I am. Yum-yum. The truth is I never loved another girl. I talked a lot, but I was fulla shit."

"I know."

"Weren't we two hot virgins, though?" Tony said. "The first time I saw you on the beach, I could see the fair hairs of your crotch. God, did peter pop! For days I went round with his hard hot head in my navel."

"What a bragger you are," Nance said. "I actually remember the moment I *knew* I loved you. When I had to say good-bye, and knew you were going north."

"Let's have a piece of tail right here."

"We're going to bed in a minute."

"But you promised me a slice in front of the radiator all winter. You puttin' me on . . . or off?"

"Noooo."

"I'll nooooaaaa you. Like Thumper said to Bambi: 'Come on down, the water's stiff.' And you do love goin' down."

"You're getting ruder."

"I got a rude cocky fella to satisfy."

"I never realized how sexy you were till you came back from the Islands."

"Gentle Jesus, I didn't know how sexy I was myself till after I'd screwed you then had to leave you. Fuck, I was the greatest five-finger man since Chopin . . . lower down, baby."

"It's draughty on the floor."

"I'll have you sweating in no time. Nice, eh? Peter loves hunting . . . specially cun'unting."

"Lift me a little, darling."

"Sweetheart, I couldn't move now even if King Kong goosed me. Ride me . . . like on a carousel."

"Shh."

"Slower . . . not like you're at a rodeo!"

"Shhhh."

"Oh, bay-bee, you got me pinned . . . keep me at your mercy. Nancy-Nancy-Nancy, Nanceeeeee . . ."

Connie is always trying to pin me and Jack down but she doesn't take her clothes off. It's usually when she's trying to make a liar out of Jackie, who, as you well know (well, you've been told often enough) is as honest as the mile is long. Jack keeps *me* on the straight and narrow when things get tight in the Great Australian Bight.

"What on earth are you thinking about when you sit there with that long face and short look, Peanut?" Mum says.

If we're not thinking about dying or being driven crazy to shooftiness by Connie we're *listening*; that's what we're doing. When Mum says somebody has a long face she means they look sad, but when she says they have a short look God knows what she means. We had a look in her mirror the first time she said this but still didn't understand about the short look, and Mum's got the cleanest biggest mirror in the house.

Connie's got this fuggy old mirror she calls an orkle. We don't know why. You'd never catch her looking in a clean mirror to see if she was tidy. She sneaks around with this crummy mirror asking it questions which she answers quick-smart herself.

Like: "Mirror, mirror, tell me honey, who's got the most money?" Straightway she gets the reply from herself in the mirror: "Connie Delarue's got more than you . . . *whoever*'s you!" Then she roars laughing, fit to kill a clown.

In me and Jack's book nothing beats . . . listening.

"Connie never listens to you," Mum said to Dad. "She's getting worse, Tony."

"That One's an angel . . . when she's in bed dead to the world," Dad said.

Connie does look like an angel when she's asleep, all wriggled up in dolly confusion. You'd never believe she could be wicked even if the Guardian Angel came in and gave you the good oil about her. She can be so awful at times I almost forget the day she was so good to Jack when I was sick.

"Being deliberately bad, Connie," Mum said, "is worse than being accidentally mean."

"I guess we're not talking about Jack Rivers," Connie said.

"Think about the good times," Jack whispered.

"I'm thinkin', I'm thinkin'." But some days they just don't seem good enough.

It's hard to believe she's always the same girl living with us. After all, it's not our fault if she's not a boy like she wants to be. I know it must be a Real Perdicament for her, but why blame Jack and me because we happen to be boys?

"Know the first thing I'd do if I *was* a boy," Connie said one day, like as if she'd never said it before.

"What's the first thing you'd do if you was a boy, Connie?" We've heard it more times than a pit whistle but you might as well hear it too.

"First thing I'd do would be to stand up right in the middle of Main Road, take me dick out, and piss all over the traffic to let everyone know. That's the first thing I'd do if I was a boy."

We can't imagine the second thing she'd do and never ask. Robin Goodfellow she'd never be. "Me and Jack wouldn't be brave enough to do that, Connie."

"It's a bloody shame You Guys *are* boys," Connie said. "You'd make a couple of nice little sheilas."

"Me and Jack don't want to be sheilas, even if I am good looking and Jack is pretty, like Mum says."

"And so shy about it?" Connie said. "But you were an ugly, funny and fumbly baby, not cute like Mum says . . . I remember that much!"

"You *were* a cute baby," Mum said. "As cute as a Kiwi chick, believe me."

And we do!

"Kiwi chick . . . hah!" Connie said. "You sure can let your head go, Woman."

"You were cute, too!" Mum grabbed Connie and force-tickled her.

Connie did laugh a bit at that but broke away and pinched my chin, saying, "Cutey-cutey Kiwi, wanna do a peewee?"

"Now, Connie," Mum said in what Dad calls her referee voice.

"Now, Nance," Connie said.

"Now, now," Dad said, coming in at the slide end.

"Now's as good a time as ever to sneak away," Jack said to me. Jack didn't mean to be sneaky about sneaking away . . . but I guess you understand what he meant. You must know by now Jack Rivers is not sneaky or shoofty in any way whatsoever.

While they were now-nowing, me and Jack went up to Mum's big mirror to see just how good looking and pretty and neat and tidy we were compared to Connie; so while we were there we thought we might as well pop it a question to see if it was a very good orkle:

> "Mirror, mirror, big and tall
> Who's the best kids in the world?"

That lovely clean mirror answered nearly as quickly as Connie's crummy little orkle:

> "Jack Rivers and his mate come first;
> Connie Delarue is sure the worst!"

Boy, is that mirror a clever mirror!

"Mum, know what? Your mirror is a better orkle than Connie's crummy mirror."

"Oracle," Mum said with a smile that was somewhere between Frisco and St. Jo. I think she might've been somewhere between fighting-gamely-the-old-onwee and the Monthlies.

13

DEEP-VEINED in the town, for half a century the Death Seat remained unheard of beyond the perimeters of the valley. By the time the travelling Thomases discovered it, it was already sanctified by time, a place where people went to talk to themselves, regardless of their fluency, their goodness or badness, their conscience, their religion.

"I know you understand, Reverend, but I just want to be alone . . . and safe from even the most sympathetic inquiries."

The lost, looking, found more than they thought they'd misplaced.

"I needed to know how far I'd wandered from those who loved me and were willing to let me be free."

The foolish who needed to believe in more than one God; the wise who believed in a religionless God; the few who believed in men; the many who believed in their Own God; the truth seekers.

"Truth is what one man believes above all else."

"Truth is what the majority believe when they are asked to decide."

"Megalomaniacs speak the truth when there are enough idiots listening."

"Listen, mate, the truth is what I believe and you don't."

The truth of the Death Seat was the hairline between loneliness and solitude.

It was a place mothers could go to when they had been unfair to a child.

"How can I feel this sorry if I think I'll do it again without knowing . . . or know that I'll do it again without thinking?"

Where husbands queried their unfaithfulness.

"It's not that I'm oversexed or that she was such a beaut screw. Guess I'm a born bastard."

Young men tried to be contrite there.

"I should have waited till we were married. Now what'll I do for an encore? The bridesmaids?"

The not so penitent.

"Number seven in a gang bang! Where's me pride? Not in me bloody pants, that's fer sure. Never again . . . unless I can be at least second or third."

It was also OK to sober up there before going home to a tongue-lashing from the missus.

" 'It's like this, luv. Me cobber got made a foreman and . . .' No . . . she'll wanna know why I wasn't made a foreman. 'There were so many fellas in the shout it took ages to . . .' No good! 'I felt crook, darl, and thought a few extra beers would . . .' Shit! I'll just tell 'er I've done it again. I'm a rotter who can't keep 'is word! She'll agree with that. Bloody women . . . they *love* weak men."

Kids went there if and when they'd been hurt by other children.

"I hate Swiftie Madison! I'll hate him till the day I die . . . even if I live to be twenty. That's if he doesn't want to get engaged when we're fifteen."

Once a very young girl called Goldie Killorn sat and dreamed there, through her duck-ugly subteens, through a beautiful sister's untimely death, waiting . . . for some fighting knight or shining farmer.

"But please, God . . . don't let him be a miner."

"Last weekend, while I was in Boomeroo, Darcy, I sat on the Death Seat for a while."

"And?"

"Decided I wasn't sorry that I was marrying you."

"If you'd decided that you *were* sorry I'd put a bomb under it."

"I also arranged a day with the minister and booked the School of Arts for the kitchen tea my mother insists on having."

"Don't tell me they still have those orgies in the country?"

"Would you believe Brueghel happenings?"

"Do we have to?"

"Yep! Sorry. For you not myself. Oh, and Jerry Kyle is going to sing 'I Bless Every Hour.' "

"Isn't his mother the local Madam?"

"You city people are so naïve."

Alice Arden Henrietta Allsop busted up to Mrs. Killorn.

"So Goldie is going to marry a man who isn't exactly a young man?"

"She's certainly marrying a man," Mrs. Killorn said. "And I wouldn't be happy if she was marrying a young man."

"Men who marry after thirty usually marry the wrong girl," Mrs. A. said, "because they've most likely met and lost the right girl before then. Or they might even be . . . you know?"

"I have no idea."

Mrs. Allsop was not taken aback. Gossip was her property.

"Not interested in us women for what we're really worth, I mean. Have you thought about that?"

"No, Alice; because I knew you'd give it enough thought for the whole town." Mrs. Killorn was a lady: a difficult reputation for a widow to maintain in a small town with lots of hide. She gave Mrs. Allsop a genteel smile and a not-so-polite nod.

Lovers know the value of the Death Seat. There they can answer their own misgivings, salve a defeat, rationalize a victory, take sanctuary from the hocussing of love.

A young bride-to-be with a last grateful prayer: "You done good, Victoria Jane; you done good! He's handsome and got a good job and all the girls are jealous . . . *and don't ever let them forget it.*"

At her kitchen tea all her green girl-friends sing congratulations in the centre of the dance floor at the School of Arts, with their tongues in their cheeks and their pussies in heat for love of their girlfriend's stud-lover, Brian.

"Oh, Jane Paulson was talked about more than she was liked really. She was only ever popular with *men.*"

"She was never a virgin. Rolled on her pacifier when she was six months old."

"Don't let it throw you, Janie. You've got a *man,* and half the women in the world are wishin' they had any prick right this minute."

A kitchen tea in Boomeroo is not a shower tea. That would be like calling the Great Coral Sea Typhoon of World War II summer rain.

Meanwhile . . . out the back of the School of Arts, gathered round the keg on the sacred stump behind the shithouse, the boys are getting pissier while the girls inside are getting kissier and hissier.

These guys can usually rustle up a song:

> *"Here's to Brian, he's a fool*
> *To let one sheila hone his tool:*
> *The Chadla molls are sheddin' tears,*
> *But he'll be back within two years."*

So drink chugga-lug, chugga-lug, chugga-lug; and eat your bachelor hearts out because your mate's gonna wake up with it laid on every morning . . . for a while, anyway.

> *"Here's to Brian . . . now he's gawn,*
> *They reckon he was born wiff a horn:*
> *The news is great to lotsa guys . . .*
> *He won't be around to screw their wives."*

So drink chugga-lug, chugga-lug, chugga-lug: and early in the morning Constable Hervey would be down to the Death Seat to unshackle Brian and take him home before he was found naked by too many people. This tradition started when a few fellows decided to rope and bind their marriage-bound pal and leave him there after they returned roaring drunk from a Chadla brothel when a kitchen tea had staggered into a stag. They had intended to leave him with his underpants on, but he begged otherwise:

"For Chrissake fellows, leave me bloodywell naked if you're goin' through with it. For once I didn't change me underpants . . . today."

"Oh, you cruddy bastard!"

So naked it was, because the Australian male, Neanderthal, Napoleonic, crude, misogynous or whatever, is not dirty. He is clean to the extent of godliness, and his mother made him so, make no mistake about that.

Unfortunately Duck Allsop was nearly always there before the policeman.

"Git away from here, ya dirty little bastard. And keep that dirty big black retriever's nose outa my arse."

"OK . . . but I'll just tickle ya balls with this bitta fern."

"So help me, Duck, if you don't fuck off I'll catch up with you tomorrow and kick shit outa both you and your fuckin' mongrel!"

Duck became the town authority on the important physical details of the newly married men.

"I tellya what," Duck said to a kick of kids, "Young Henry Garside's got a prick like a German sausage. An' it was so stiff, if it'da been Monday morning Miss Bowen woulda mistook it for the flagpole and run up the Union Jack."

"I hear Ben Leslie's onto Young 'Enery's wife now. What could he give 'er Young 'Enery ain't got?"

"Finesse?"

"That some kinda French fuck?"

"Be sure you don't leave any hairs in the soap, Mr. Leslie," Young Henry's satisfied wife said.

"Oh, for Godsake call me Ben," Ben Leslie said. "I've been up you all afternoon. A long fuck is as good an introduction as anything."

"It's just that your hair's a different colour to Henry's and mine."

"Come here, you prim little whore," Ben said, "and get some pubic hair in your teeth."

Young Henry's wife was good at loving, better at honouring, but best at obeying.

"Nibble my foreskin, darling," Ben said like a detached scene director. He flexed his toes to hurry his third ejaculation. "Swallow it this time." He held her head at a very uncamera angle.

Young Henry's wife was not afraid or ashamed. She knew the Death Seat assimilated and protected anything that was part of the flux of humanity . . . even if she didn't know what that meant. Nobody could ask for more.

It is a place that belongs to men, women, and children, and it is a good place. A place that many gods would be pleased to acknowledge.

14

LAST CHRISTMAS Jack Rivers had a Christmas card from Santa Claus — we must be growing up because once we used to call him Daddy Christmas — and this made Connie hopping mad, honestly. Who knows why? It was a real card in a real envelope with the Queen's stamp on it and was delivered by the postman like as if penny-whistles were on sale at Woolworths for a halfpenny.

"I think a pillowslip for *both* Those Boys is just a clever way for a certain person to get double for Christmas," Connie said. "And I'm surprised that Santa Stupid Claus hasn't woke up to it. I ought to put him wise." She raved on and on.

"I like it better when you're galavanting round town out of my hair," Mum said.

"Santa hates greedy gutses!" Connie said. "Like those kinky kids that go into town and sit on his wobbly knee and ask for everything in the toy factory run by those 'andy 'elpin' dumb elves who never get paid. Bet they've got nothing in their rotten money boxes. Well, I'm sure glad I'm rich and got *power*."

All this time she was giving me and Jackie the deadeye.

"Listen, Puss," Mum said finally. "If you don't pipe down Santa will be leaving you nil in your pillowslip. Go hang up two pillowslips yourself if it will make you feel better."

Dad came in at the wrong moment . . . again, and started off. "Why a pillowslip? Why a goddamn pillowslip? When I was a little jasper in Fin'lee, Oh-hi-ho, we hung up socks. And mighty little ones, too!" He was strutting up and down like the Chief Elf at the North Pole.

"Please don't go into all that again," Mum said. "You know very well by now that the kids here hang up pillowslips instead of socks." She pitter-pattered her voice softly like Mrs. Claus warming Santa's own socks before he harnessed the reindeer for the long trip to bring Joy to the World . . . like they sing at church.

I know Connie can be fun when she imitates Dad sometimes: "Why a pillowslip? When I was a little jasper in Oh-ho-hoh! we hung up mighty little socks . . . even bloody little socks . . . sometimes with holes in 'em!" It wouldn't be Connie if she didn't overdo it; but she sure can strut like Dad when he goes on . . . when the Yanks are coming to divide the world between Frisco and St. Jo.

"What's a jasper, Connie?"

"Aw . . . probably some little Yankee drongo."

She is a card when she wants to be and can have me and Jack in stitches at times. But she wasn't much of a Joker this day last Christmas. She was more like a Knave. She kept nagging till Dad did his block, lock-stock-and-barrel. And when Daddy does his block, lock-stock-and-barrel — blue-eyes or no Daddy-blue-eyes — you can throw out the whole darn pack of cards.

"You all heah gimme some shush and *hear this*," Dad roared, flinging his newspaper at the Christmas tree and making the angel dance.

"Don't do your loll, doll," Mum said.

"This settles it," Dad said. "Now listen . . . there's to be one pillowslip per person to each bed . . . and that is it!" Talk about angry.

"Ah has spoken," Mum said angrier-er-ililly. She was mad, too.

"Now upstairs, Peanut, and quit that bum-mumbling to your mate or I'll git up onto the roof and personally shoot Santa down. And Connie, git your piano practice over with and then to bed . . . you've been playing that Minute Waltz for twenty bloody minutes."

As Mum would say: He was being his very worst Ausmerican self . . . which isn't himself.

Connie grinned slyly and yukked her teeth at us. They needed a good brushing as usual.

"You have the pillowslip, Peanut," Jack said to me.

"No, you have the pillowslip, Jack," I said.

Dad threw the newspaper, which he'd just picked up, down again and yelled, "I told you to quit that bloody mumbling!"

Mum sprang after him like she was going to race him somewhere because she knew as we did what was going to be the outcome: The Good Old Whoosh from the Flying Fingers. "Don't hit him, Tony," she said.

I looked up at Daddy like I do when I want him to think I'm falling to pieces and one whack will Humpty Dumpty me. Sometimes it works . . . sometimes it doesn't.

"Even Phar Lap lost a few," Connie says.

Both me and Mum lost this time. Dad walloped me hard three times. He hit me and hit hard. Real wrappers. Rappers? Across the back of the legs where it hurts like billyo, but I didn't cry because I thought Santa wouldn't want to find me with giveaway tears in my eyes like as if I'd been crying for more toys. I told you I'm being clever these days.

"So help me God, Peanut. This is *it*," Dad said. And that *it* boiing-boiinged upstairs and downstairs and in my-lady's-chamber, wherever that may be. "I'll rip that sonofabitch friend of yours apart, from Frisco to St. Jo, if I hear his name in this house again."

Mum pushed past Dad and slapped him with her own handy newspaper.

"It's Christmas, Tony," Mum said. "Get off Jack's back. How can you hate him at Christmas?"

"I don't hate him, Nance," Dad cried. "I just get sick and tired of hearing about him."

Connie was thumping the piano like as if old Mr. Marks the piano tuner from Nulla Nulla was counting time across the creek. If that was the Minute Waltz, Jack and me are eight-day clocks. She was donging away like Big Ben striking midnight on the wireless when Inspector Scott of Scotland Yard comes on, banging as if Saul Hamilton was listening and she wanted him to know she hated him as badly as she plays . . . which is plenty badly. Bandy-Andy could play better with his crippled hand. Connie is what Mum calls a Chopstick-Chopper and Grandma Leo calls a Drummer-Thrummer. Why they pay good money to have her play so bad is a misery of mystery.

"Are you jealous of Jack?" Mum said to Dad.

"Oh, fer Chrissake!" Dad said. "How the hell would I know that? Maybe I am. I do love Peanut, you know. What's left of him after you and Jack Rivers take your shares."

"Go to bed, Boys," Mum said. "I'll be up to tuck you in in a minute."

"He is my son, Nance," Tony said, standing at the foot of the stairs, looking at her as though she had robbed a hidden bank in his heart. "I should mean more to him than I seem to. But . . . *hell* . . . I don't hate his little mate. True, he gets on my nerves a bit . . . and Peanut is a pain in the ass sometimes on the subject of Jack, but I sure as hell don't hate him."

"Then quit riding him," Nance said.

"That's a laugh. Jack is so bloody unbroken even a Skuthorpe couldn't ride him." Their eyes were still sparring.

"I let you have Connie," Nance said, "because I felt when you came back from the war you had those years to make up. But all you've turned out is a cast iron little girl. And all I wanted was a sweet daughter I could dress the pants off."

"You better make sure you haven't got one in Peanut, Nance. It's a tough world, honey!"

"They don't have to have a tough babyhood just because you did."

They stood at ungiving angles.

"I was telling the truth about my boyhood. You know I wasn't *complaining* about it."

"I know." Nance was thinking of lonely pleasures she had enjoyed without this man whose love afflicted her. "But please let Peanut grow up in his own infant time. Everything else in the world is passing so fast, Tony."

"You're a clinger, Nance. What makes you think he'll want to let go of you later?"

She took a dizzy breath. "I promise you, Tony."

"You're the one always saying boys will be boys, Nance. But boys will be what they're encouraged to be. Make no doubts about that!"

"That doesn't mean they should be robbed of their childhood . . . and have their growing minds stripped of imagination."

Tony finally relaxed his veined grip on the stairway. He

noticed Connie at the piano when he went back to the lounge where he flopped. "You seem to be the expert." He cast that aside. "Hey . . . Connie, up to bed, *Big-ears!*"

Nance flicked her lips at Connie. It was meant to be a smile but wasn't, so she patted her reassuringly instead.

Halfway up the stairs, Connie turned and said, "Good night, You Two!"

"Good night . . ."

". . . Connie."

They looked at each other wordlessly for a long time before Tony said, "She's not all that tough. She's ninety-nine per cent act. She's a whole circus of kids in one pair of jeans."

"Where you put her," Nance said. "You don't really understand what I mean." She collected his newspaper and took it to him, wondering if it was Professor Higgins's slippers.

"I know what you *mean*, but I'm not sure I understand . . . or care. I don't think we know any more than any parents. All we're doing is learning to live with our kids as surely as they're learning to live with us."

"I only meant that . . ."

". . . I made a mess of Connie, so hands off Peanut?"

"No."

"Oh, Nance, how innocent your innocence is! You compare these kids to your long-lost Mitch Singleton. Worse. With your memory of him. But these are my kids, not Mitch Singleton's. I think the only one of them who'll ever resemble Mitch is Jack Rivers . . . in *your* imagination. Come on now, don't sniffle. You know I can't stand weeping women and you're not basically a wailer, anyhow. I accepted the fact that you loved Mitchell Singleton more than you loved me . . ."

"No!"

". . . yes, and it's OK. Not just because he's dead. Loving him got you ready for me. Oh God, Nance, you know I'd rip my own tongue out rather than hurt you or the kids." He drew her close. "Fuck! I sound like Big Sister. Look, you married me because Mitch Singleton didn't come back from the war. Right?"

Nance nodded. "Oh Tony, I wanted to die . . . but I didn't. It's not that easy to die."

"Not when you really don't want to. It's OK . . . here, wipe your bloody eyes. I'll go upstairs and say I'm sorry . . . to *everybody*. Like you said, it's Christmas. Hey!"

"What?"

"Doan say *wot* say *ay*," Tony said, pulling her down beside himself. "Can I say just a little more?"

Nance nodded. More times than necessary.

"Maybe I don't approve of sensitive basstids . . . and I don't approve of brash little girls, either. But we're both wrong. Everybody has a right to their own roadshow . . . so to get to the witty-pity, don't you think you might be a bit too . . . protective of Peanut, and that Connie just might (mind you) be a little bit jealous of your trio? You, Jack and Peanut. Without knowing she's jealous. You don't pay her a lot of mind. She might want to love you more than you're letting her. Shit!"

He was on his feet again, standing in front of her like evidence in tight jeans. Nance's nirvana he was not. He was thinking of the time an analyst in New Guinea had asked him if he was active or passive. Asked him? Tony Delarue, who had screwed a swath between Cincinnati and Cleveland . . . who enjoyed every latitude of sex . . .

"Me? I'm prejudiced because of one bum analyst. But, prejudiced or willing, I still don't understand psychological crap. Connie *might* think a lot more about the things she doesn't rave on about. Hell! Say something, Nance."

She reached up and touched the wedding band she had finally talked him into wearing. Shyness was not a Nance thing, but she found it cleansing.

"About the pillowslips," Tony said, lifting her to meet his body. "I'll hang one for Jack Rivers at the foot of our bed, and . . . I'll square it with Connie. We'll tell Peanut they can come into our room as soon as they think Christmas morning has come."

"How abart that?" Nance said.

I suppose after ratting her down I should also tell you that Connie can be as . . . Stupendice as the ice cream man when she *flies*. It's like the rest of the world stops when it's flying time; it gives us a mighty thrill when we hear her shout.

"Hey! You Boys help me get me flying doovers out and on. I'm flying today!"

"Flying today! Did you hear that, Jack? Things are merry in Londonderry all right. Coming, Connie. Coming right away." I get so excited it makes me want to pee.

After all the fixing mending strapping taping glueing and grunting, there is Connie with her wings stuck onto Grandma Leo's old corsets. Like a bird that's been caught up in a 'lastic factory and escaped without its feathers. Little birds that see her get such a shock they quit flying and fall, like the sparrows in the hymn, but I don't think they meet God's tender view. I'm sure Connie doesn't and she often falls farther than she flies. I think those little birds that see Connie flapping die of hawkshock.

"Magnificent," Mum said. "Be careful. I still don't like the idea . . . even if you do it beautifully."

"Barnstorming again," Dad said as if he was a Famous Father.

"Barnstorming, my eye," Connie said after he disappeared. "I'm skystorming and God had better beware He don't get a wing in His eye."

"You're Stupendice, Connie."

"I'm more'n that," Connie said. "I'm stupendenormous. Stand back there, little folk! I'm gonna fly. Connie the Great's gonna fly again."

"Look, Jack. Look where Connie is. They'll think Bert Hinkler's back in Boomeroo."

"Stand back, kids. I'm nearly ready. Just getting me flyin' breath. How d'ya like me new wings? There's more brown paper in this lot than's left in the Store to wrap parcels. Now watch. I'm gonna fly from the top of the garage up here to the manure heap in the back garden."

Oh, Connie! You're fantiflicating. Mighty Connie Delarue . . . our Sister. The Best of the Few. The gamest goddamn flyer in Boomeroo.

"Amy Johnson and Amelia Earhart will never see which way my tail went."

"Smiffie will want to marry you, Connie."

"Shut up, yous; I'm promotin' meself," Connie said. "Just watch. Next year I'm gonna sell tickets and You Two will get in free for bein' a good audience . . . if you don't get too carried away. Here . . . I . . . go!"

Me and Jack love this getting ready part the most because it lasts longer. To tell the truth, the flying is almost over before we know it's begun.

"Fly, Connie, fly!"

"I'm greater than Mermoz!"

We know this.

"Better than Lindbergh!"

He must know this by now.

"Even the birds are jealous."

Well, they're still dying from shock.

"You look like a lost, school-concert Aztec," Mum said once — whatever that may be — and Connie never spoke to her for three days, and only then to borrow her best scissors for new wings.

"The crowds are yelling for more."

"I seen more people watching a dog piss," Duck Allsop said one day. He copped it from Connie's flying feet a few days later when she ambushed him with her wings on and landed smack on top of him.

But she does fly. Sometimes from the back steps' high landing to the manure heap — and that's farther than from the garage. Wings flapping. Arms grabbing the air. Corsets creaking. Feet going sixteen to the dozen. Her voice whooshing like the wind. And for all those piddly-tingling seconds she is a flying God. It makes you feel . . . shrinky. And if Jack and me lie on the ground Connie seems to be flying higher than she knows.

We hug her when she lands, don't we, Jackie? We don't care if she smells like horses' poo or cow wee. We adore her.

"I'm gonna do it again, kids. Help me brush this horse-shit off."

"Are you hurt, Connie?"

"Hell, no! I'm like Ben Hall. It took twenty-seven bullets to kill him."

"Take me with you, *please!*"

"Peanut . . . Mum'd larrup me within an inch of me life if I took you up."

"But I'm game, Connie. I'm game."

"I know."

"You're only sayin' that! But I *am*. I'm tired of bein' un-important. I want to be like Ben Hall and Hinkler. Now! Not when I'm seven. I don't wanta wait till the lights go on . . . and you know I'm going to die young."

"I know no such thing an' don't want to hear that rub-bish," Connie said. "But I tellya what'll do: I'll take Jack for a spin."

"Oh, you are wonderful. We love you."

"OK. So don't mush all over me. Come on, Jack. Let's see what *you're* made of."

I do think that Connie might understand Jack more than Mum does . . . deep down. After Jack proved he was game we sat under the oleanders eating licorice all-sorts, and drinking lolly-water till we fair busted . . . out of my money.

"God, I'm full as a goog," Connie said. "Now help me out of this gear. I bet Leo had these corsets before Cook."

"Was Grandma Leo a convict, Connie? Is that what con-victs had to wear in the good old days?"

"Leo is a grandmother . . . ours. And grandmas can't be put in jail because they have grandchildren to send presents to, who might need them at the drop of a hat . . . or the sound of the bell when parents start fighting. It's their duty to tell parents off when they start going bad."

"How do parents go bad, Connie?"

"Spending too much time fighting over where the money goes. It should all go in the bank! Then the kids run away to their grandmas, and she moves in and gives the parents the old One-Two."

"Mum said Leo is a breed of her own."

"Yeah, because she ran away instead of us."

"Will Mum and Dad go bad for sure?"

"The kids at school reckon it happens all the time. Except to Monte Howard: he's lucky and lives with his grandfather."

"I'll be going to school soon."

"You should have gone when you were five. You're

nearly six . . . too old to be just starting. Has Mum said anything special about you going to school?"

"Like what special?"

I pretended I had licorice in my throat and wheezed a bit.

"What I can't say for fear of hurting You-Know-Who's feelings."

We pretended to be dumb-dumbs, Jack and me, but we knew what she was getting at . . . about Jack Rivers maybe going to school, too.

Later that night we heard her Having-It-Out with Mum and Dad, and if Connie Has-It-Out with you . . . pow! It might as well be happening in the middle of Main Road.

"Well, one of you parents had better tell him the facts of school life. It ain't fair letting him go to school blindfolded to get hurt. Those kids in that killer playground will murder Jack Rivers."

"Perhaps you *had* better say something, Tony."

"Not on your life me," Dad said.

"Oh, I'm sure it will be all right," Mum said. "Children are not *that* cruel."

"Mad dogs ain't angels," Connie said. "Kids are crueller than You Parents wanta remember."

We can hear Mum getting up now. That means morning is here. Dad will yawn right through the wall and then he'll yelp . . . it sounds like somebody gave him a little lovey whack. After that he'll scratch himself. If we're up early we see him scratching that hairy patch around his dick. Then he flump-flumps to the bathroom.

"I'm glad I got a hairy man . . . they send me."

"Where to, Mum?"

"Darling," Mum said. "Didn't know you were up."

"Jeeze!" Dad will say. "Whoever invented morning

should have his head shaved to the brain and his pissy horn tooled down."

Connie won't wake up till she sniffs the toast, but you know all about that. "Jeeze . . . I bet those Forty Basstids invented waking up." Then she'll fling her pillow at us. What a throw she's got!

"Like one of Larwood's," Mum said.

"Who the hell's Larwood when he's home for breakfast?" Dad said.

"A famous English bowler," Mum said.

"Nine- or ten-pin?" Dad said.

"Cricket — "

"Goddamn! Do they bowl in that game, too?"

"I feel too jiggered to start the day," Connie said. "Too pooped out to listen to their jazz."

"Like in poop, Connie?"

"No, like in buggered-before-I-begin."

"Jack Rivers and me are never buggered-before-we-begin. 'Cause we cuddle up to each other. You want Jack to sleep with you some night, Connie?"

"Wouldn't that rope the bulls if the kids at school found out I slept with Jack Rivers?" Connie shuddered. "Imagine what they'd be writing on the fences."

Jack Rivers and me have slept a long time together and we've never roped any bulls. I bet lots of boys and their mates sleep together. Men too! And Dad's buddy died in his arms.

"Gee, Jack, what a lovely way to die . . . in Dad's arms."

"Dyin' ain't exactly as much fun as community singing," Connie said. "If you want the truth, the whole truth and nothing but the truth."

"That sounds good . . . like dying three times."

"Well, it ain't all," Connie said, suddenly on her high horse. And they don't come any higher. "Dyin' is like having to sit and listen to Mrs. Upsa Downey sing 'There's a New Star in Heaven Tonight' at a kitchen tea . . . and all the old biddies crying in their shandies over Rudolph Valentino . . . Whoever he was, he's lucky he can't bloody hear Mrs. Upsa singing that song about him."

"Mum said he's dead."

"That song musta killed him," Connie said. I tell you she's getting quicker with rip-snorting replies.

"All the Downeys have strong voices," Mum said.

"Mrs. Upsa is a Limburger among voices," Dad said.

Jack Rivers and me like her singing "There's a New Star in Heaven Tonight." When I get my bike I might ride over to Wollondonga and ask Mrs. Upsa if she'll sing it when I die . . . before they post me to heaven.

And I don't care if you say I said that: I'm getting sick of keeping secrets about dying.

15

BOOMEROO DRINKERS loved one another in that awesome eclectic way only Australian blokes can love men in their dirty ceremonies of strange innocence, filling the abyss between their ideas and imagination with insults. In argument they were harder to catch than soap in sudsy water.

"The on'y Awesome I know is Awesome Wells, an' 'e don't know nothing 'bout 'lectricity."

When Darcy landed in the buzzing Sulphide bar he felt Goldie had prepared one of those revolting, gluey flypaper mats especially for him.

"You must be that guy came up from Sydney to photograph the Death Seat for the *Women's-bloody-Weekly*."

"Well, the spread I'm doing is for a commercial quarterly, but if it's good they'll resell it. This assignment's more . . . relative than professional, for me!"

"You want a beer or are you too sophisticated to drink piss?"

"I drink beer. Do you think it's a compliment to call someone sophisticated, or are you being sarcastic?"

"I thought it meant that you'd sorta . . . been around."

"So what kind of guy are you if you're not fuckin' sophisticated?"

"Ordinary. With a few bad habits you wouldn't want to know about." Darcy had an impelling feeling that he'd been set up. Bloody-busy-body-Goldie.

"Oh, we're great bastards for learnin', mate."

"So . . . I have a lot of stupid faults and make a lot of stupid mistakes. How's that for openers . . . mate?"

"You'll pass in a scrum."

"You have been around, but?"

"Some."

"What d'ya remember most?"

"That I never got to the top of the Empire State Building in New York."

"My father-in-law's been to the top of the Ethel Tower."

"Your father-in-law's never been past Big Fat Nellie's shack. His prick wears his shoes."

"Here, let me buy this round."

"Your turn'll come. We've all got hands and pockets round here . . . except Big Grub."

"I pay my way!"

"You wouldn't shout a moll a packet of Condy's Crystals."

"Well, mate . . . what d'ya think of us?"

"You're putting me on."

"No! You come to do the Death Seat. Take photographs of our town. Come in here for a beer. You might be laughin' at us for all we know."

"You wouldn't be buying me a bloody beer if you thought that."

"OK. So are we . . . whatya'call-it . . . relative?"

"Insofar as I want to . . ."

"Watch it, matey!"

". . . amplify the difference between city and country."

"Well, what did you think of Kincomba?"

"Neither city nor country. I hated the place."

"You could drink all day here on that."

Kincomba was a busy snooty town . . . the navel of the valley; but for all its push and petty, money-mattering propaganda it didn't deceive Lillipillians. They knew all about Kincomba and its Cucumber citizens. Like all characterless, plate-faced people who lived in big towns and cities they seldom knew their neighbour's name, let alone any of his business. They are worldwide but in Kincomba (unlike in real cities) they speak with Australian accents of which they seem proud to be ashamed, and think with Australian reasoning of which they are overbearingly aware.

Darcy heaved his breath. He had discovered something he could survive the afternoon on.

"They're a bit like Yanks, ya know," someone said.

"Sure, but Americans already have what most Cucumbers still want," Darcy said. "More of everything!"

"You might be right there, mate. Don'tya wanta schooner insteada a middie?"

"OK." Darcy was quite happy to let the rabidity of the rest of the world go by.

"They got a bloody woman on the Council down there now, you know. In Kincomba!"

"She's got 'er fuckin' problems cut out."

"Ever been to one of them Council meetings?"

"No. I hear enough shit on the radio."

"Gentlemen! Gentlemen!" Councillor Duxmann said loudly . . . meaning: Shut up. "And my dear Mrs. Cathcart, can we get back to the matter at hand which is not juvenile drinking? Sooner or later we have to take the gravel out of the Terribana Hills and face the opposition of the Northside towns."

"We'll lose support from the miners. They still do a bit of hunting there," young Councillor Craig said.

"If Rome had thought that way Michelangelo wouldn't have had his marbles," Duxmann said.

"Really, Councillor, your metaphors get more meaningless every meeting," Mrs. Lucy Cathcart said, immediately sorry and wondering if she should have said similes.

"Look at it nearer home," old Councillor Moroney said. "If they hadn't taken the Gosford stone out of *their* hills we wouldn't have any of the beautiful vaults we have in Kincomba Cemetery."

"A small white wooden cross is all a Serviceman gets," said Councillor Thurston.

"Men who die for their countries aren't the ostentatious types."

"Men who go to war to die for their countries are fools."

UPROAR. Both in the Council and the pub. Who said that, where?

"Gentlemen! Gentlemen!" Duxmann shouted. He loved uproars: you could accomplish so much while others were uproaring. "Let's get back to taking the gravel out of the Terribana Hills by . . ."

". . . hook or by crook. That's how they'll get it out. Blind Freddie can see that."

"So you care? I didn't see you replantin' any trees when you cleared your allotment."

"Up your Oxford Pass, mate!"

"They won't even serve you a beer in Kincomba if they think you're still goin' to school . . . since that Mrs. Cathcart's been on the Council. She's a total-tea bitch."

The Kincomba Council (you might as well know because you're going to find out the first time you have a beer in the Sulphide pub at Boomeroo) pinches the profits from the valley mines and factories and farms in devious ways. More blatantly steals from small businesses, professionals and oldtime craftsmen . . .

"Oldtime crafts? That's a laugh."

"I don't know. Big Fat Nellie's son, Black Rupert, still makes boomerangs."

"And Nellie's still makin' men outa young boys!"

"What you do think about women havin' important jobs, mate?"

"What's he think about *women?*"

Darcy was sure there had to be an acceptable ten bob answer to this million pound question, but the beer and their obvious genuine interest in his opinions were simmering him. "I think . . . that women have been forced into an artificial mould through the centuries . . . a more insignificant mould than they would have chosen for themselves."

There was a silence more tinny than golden.

"Hey . . . wait a minute . . . you're the bastard goin' to marry Goldie Killorn, I bet. Ain'tya?"

"Me, the bastard."

"BeJesus. Glad we haven't got round to Ben Leslie this arvo."

"Matter of fact, I expected his name to be thrown into the ragbag any minute."

"So what's your fuckin' name?"

"Darcy Hall."

"OK, Ben . . . you tell us grubs if we're missin' anything. After all, we know all we've got to go on about is the biggest bloody rock in the world and the Sydney Harbour Bridge."

"You have far more than that. You have . . . Winchester, paddling on a shoal of Dooragul Creek where Fenian green silky oaks and golden green camphor laurels wade."

"And across the railway line that fuckin' eyesore, the Kincomba Stockyard and Abattoir."

"An' Duxmann's Knackery."

"If you live in Winchester you might as well breathe through your arse."

"You've got Nulla Nulla. They say it grows the best tomatoes in the state. The Meteorologic Bureau reckons it's protected from frosts all year."

"But it ain't protected from the Kincomba Tomato Board!"

"What've meteors got to do with the weather?"

"What the hell are meteors?"

"Those flamin' things from outa space."

"Russian or American?"

"Buy me a beer an' I'll tell you what Nostradamus said about them," Big Grub said.

"You wouldn't know fuckin' Nostra-anybody from your fuckin' nostril, you livid-fuckin'-liar!"

"Anyway . . . Nulla Nulla grows the freshest biggest bloodiest tomatoes in New South Wales, the bloody biggest fresh State of the Commonwealth."

"What kind of dumbarse country is a damn Commonwealth, Ben?"

"A country where everything's common except the wealth," Darcy said. "Where the rich are filthy rich and the poor are cleaned."

"You've even got Pinhead in."

"It's what makes one individual happy that counts. When did you last look up at the bloody Milky Way? You could travel till your arse aches in the northern hemisphere and never see anything remotely like it."

"I'll buy that. But if you try to tell us Wollondonga is relative to anything on this bloody earth you're in strife."

"Never been there."

"Born lucky, see!"

"It's where the Sanitary Depot is, just across the creek."

"Wollbung Charlie still sells most of his big Spanish onions in Kincomba, but."

Wollbung Charlie was the last of the Chinese market gardeners in the district and grew his vegetables on the perimeter of the area designated for the ditches dug to bury the shit from the up-valley towns.

"And what *did* you think of the Death Seat?"

"It was drizzling this morning, remember: I took a few shots of it wet. Then the sun came out. The effect was superb. The dazzling skin of the rain peeling away in the sunlight . . . I think I caught what I wanted . . . I . . . talk too much!"

"No the fuck you don't. Go on. We get browned off with our own braggin'. What about Boomeroo?"

"I think . . . it's too real to be a . . . picture-postcard place." Darcy cursed Goldie between thoughts. "It belongs too much to you to ever be . . . calendarized."

"An' you're gonna marry Goldie Killorn?"

"As you said, born lucky."

"Half the bloody town'll be at the kitchen tea, you know."

"I've been warn . . . told."

"And we'll take you to Chadla when the kegs go dry."

"OK. Goldie said I had to make it in Boomeroo . . . or else."

"Tell 'er some of the Bulls are givin' you a stag. Ever been to Chadla?"

"No, never."

"You'll wish you never had."

"I'll look forward to it."

"You'll bloodywell look back on it, too, you city bastard."

"Wish we had time to take you on a pub crawl in Bora Bora."

"Bora's got more pubs an' mines than houses."

Darcy reported dutifully to Goldie. "Well, I spent the afternoon drinking with some of the Boomeroo Bulls after I finished photographing the Death Seat."

"Still want to marry me?"

"I think so."

"What did you talk about?"

"Kincomba."

"That's average."

"Women in important jobs."

"In the Sulphide pub?"

"Yep! And I assured them that you were neither important nor about to go into politics. We discussed where a man might be most happy if not in Boomeroo. Of course, I did most of the dissing and they did all the cussing. And they never gave me a chance to go for one piss all afternoon. Bloody lot of camels."

"What's the rest of the rub in the pub?"

"Everything's relative unless you're sentenced to life in Wollondonga . . . and I think I'm an accepted bastard."

"I love accepted bastards," Goldie said, knighting his nose with one slender finger.

"And I love you because you are not as complicated as you look but as bright as a woman should allowably be . . . hereabouts."

"Thank you. And what do you think of Boomeroosters?"

Darcy stifled a half-throated reaction. "I . . . that's a lousy question . . . but . . . I like the way they avail themselves of a local brewed humour to ignore or belittle what ugliness might surround them. Oh, and I'll be taken to Chadla after the kitchen tea."

"Lucky bucky!"

"Where the hell is Chadla; and who or what is Bora Bora?"

"Chadla, my sweet, is a rejuvenated Army town where the best whores charge the most. Bora is a true mining town, right out of the heart of Wales, terraces and all . . . and shafted more than Oscar Wilde."

"Miss Killorn?"

"You could say dug deeper than the Army molls in Chadla."

"I love your local self," Darcy said.

"I'll settle for the way you see me in the lens of your camera. And don't ever try to enlarge the image more than the grain allows."

"Sweetheart, I'll be very very chary till I have you completely in focus."

"What? Are you gonna focus now?"

"I've heard that Scotch joke."

"Well, the way I see it, mate," Goldie began, swaying her head like a not-too-bright Pinhead.

Darcy grabbed her and held her in a chauvinistic mate-hug and, before kissing her, said in a Boomeroo Bull voice, "Listen . . . you couldn't see a fuckin' fly at a butcher's picnic, you bloody grub."

16

AFTER THE INQUISITION while Nance was at the Store — and after her trip of self-judgment to the graffiti culvert — Connie kept out of The Boys' way for the rest of the day. It passed torturously slowly for Peanut and Jack Rivers. They even argued. Peanut said how vile Connie was, but Jack reminded him of the nice ways she had when she had them: the soul of the matter being that Jack was inclined to believe Connie's saying kids like Duck Allsop could make school hell for him . . .

"Fancy having Duck Allsop skitch his dirty big black retriever onto you on the way home from school when nearly every kid in town was milling along Main Road."

. . . whereas Peanut resolutely believed Jack could have overcome all. Could have; for it was already resolved.

Nance was busy covering textbooks with coloured paper and transfers, and sorting out summer clothes from the woollens soon to be stored away, but Peanut, releasing Jack for the first time ever to his own quandary, would not let her be.

"Why am I so little, Mum? It'll take forever for me to be ten. How come I wasn't born before I was? Why didn't you pick me up at the same time you picked Connie up? Didn't you want me then? Why, Mum, why? Aren't you ever gonna answer me, Mum?"

"If you stop interrogating me and give me half a chance, I'll try," Nance said.

Right then Tony came in (naturally) and said, "What's all the flapdoodle about, Goober? I could hear your voice all the way up the stairs."

"Oh," Nance said, "suddenly he wants to grow up yesterday."

"You should've taken lessons from the Fearless One," Tony said to his son.

"I want to be big," Peanut said, knowing his father was referring to Connie, not Jack.

"It ain't all that much," Tony said.

Peanut left it at that, satisfied to be able to add one more word to his vocabulary . . . *Inter-gating.*

That night after Peanut had kissed his mother good night and saluted his father as he sometimes did, Antony mentioned school in a matter of fact way.

"Tomorrow's the big day, eh?"

"Yes, Daddy."

"You do want to go, kiddo?"

"I'm looking forward to school, Dad. Connie said I should've gone nearly a year ago when I was five."

There was a silence as though the clocks were disoriented. Tony and Nance exchanged woeful (baleful?) looks. "How about a good-night kiss for me tonight?" Tony said. "You'll say you're too big for that sort of thing once you start school."

"No, I won't," Peanut said and kissed him blissfully. "Dad?"

"Yeah, mate?"

"Do those big boats you showed us in Sydney one day still go all over the world?"

"Sure do! And we're all gonna take one to the States one day. Jack too," Dad said.

"Oh, Daddy!" The chirpy voice was lost in shock, and the squirrel eyes burned in a blaze of amazement. "Do you really love Jack?"

Antony drew Peanut into the harbour of his knees, and rested a broad weapon of a hand on the soft-haired head.

Connie's piano-tude increased.

"Listen, Junior," Tony said. "Like your fingers say: you can count on me. I love you all, and if anybody hurts one piece of my family I'll rip 'em apart, so help me . . . and you know where."

"From Frisco to St. Jo!"

"You better believe it."

Connie stopped plonking, chewed her lips and listened.

"I'm glad, Dad," Peanut said, hopped away, then added, "Good night, Mum."

" 'Night, Boys."

Connie watched The Boys go upstairs before her slaughtering fingers went back to poor Sinding, playing twice as many notes as he ever wrote for "Rustle of Spring," twice as fast as her despairing teacher would have believed her capable, and with an energy approaching a winter storm.

Peanut and Jack floated, their satisfaction filling them lighter than air, intoxicating their imaginations.

In spite of an avalanche of school-kid prayers and curses, the first day of school was not lost in some other time or any mass of flame.

"Mum," Connie said impatiently. "Second bell's gone."

"Ready in a minute."

"You said that when first bell went. You're just afraid to let go of him."

"All right, Connie! We are ready now. Did you arrange to meet Peanut and Jack at playtime to make sure they're settling in?"

Connie grabbed for words that would not make a lie. "I told Peanut where to wait for me."

"I won't be there," Peanut said. "I'll make friends with other little drongos."

"Connie, have you been using that word again?"

"No, Mother. But what other word is there? That's what they're called in Kinder."

"I don't mind, Mum," Peanut said, strangely equable. "I've made up my mind to be a good little drongo so that next year I can sort out my adjectives and adverbs."

"I will be there, just the same," Connie said, to make her alley good. "Look for me. And if any kids bother you tell 'em you're my brother. Tell them if they make trouble for you I'll . . ."

"No need to elaborate," Nance said. "We get the trend and haven't got time for the gore."

"Well, my name means something at school," Connie insisted. "He might as well know he can rely on it."

"I've got Dad behind me," Peanut said aggressively.

Nance's heart pinched her.

"You'll learn, buster," Connie said.

"I'll never need Big Myrtle Worfington behind me," Peanut said.

The preparatory excitment and commotion over, Nance became aware of the flares behind these flickerings.

"Tell me! What's going on, heah?" she said, Antony-like.

"Nothing," the kids answered together, too obligatory not to be noticeable. Their division in tone dobbed them in more than the one conspiratorial word.

Nance looked for Jack Rivers. It was strange; something

was missing. She kneeled in front of Peanut, willing to scrabble for the rag of this tension if she couldn't find the bone. "Where's Johnnie?"

"We *will* be late," Connie said quietly.

"Where is he?" Nance demanded.

Peanut couldn't answer his mother's fear as bravely as he had faced his own disaster.

"He's gone, Mumma," Connie said, inadvertently using a long-gone baby word.

Swinging round on her knees, Nance grabbed her daughter. "But *where* is he?"

"He hadda go."

"*You* sent him away."

"No, Mum . . ."

Reading his mother's inchoate intention even before she drew back an arm, Peanut said, "Don't, Mummy!" Nance swiped Connie across the face with the back of four flush fingers.

"Oh, Mum . . . don't!" Peanut cried.

"You jealous little swine," Nance said, as Connie staggered. "You can go. Don't wait for us. I see why you've been anxious to get going."

"I did it for him," Connie said, biting her mouth. "I thought you'd understand."

The deckle-edged words were too painful for Nance to absorb: the damage of distrust was between them.

Connie picked up her school bag and left, knowing it was useless to look back at an invisible mistake.

Peanut closed his eyes. What a hero she was, this sister who had conquered the world in a baggy pair of past-blue jeans and Laura Eva Oxford's corsets! Who had enough brave-gravy in her gut to strip down at the pump house and jump into the creek years before just to prove to Monte Howard and his gang that she *could* swim, even though she had never been out of her depth on the sand-bank before. His sister . . . Connie Hinkler Delarue, a flyer made for everlasting sunsets. Amelia Earhart in dreams.

"I'll larrup her personally when she comes home," Nance said.

"No!" Peanut shouted his protest, his eyes still unopen.

"Where is Jack?" His mother asked.

"He went after breakfast to catch the Express," Peanut said, opening his to look beyond his mother's tragic eyes. "I can hear it bellowing up the valley from Kincomba now, can't you? Jack is going Outback, Mum. To drove for a while. Then he's going to the Islands and New Guinea to see Grandma Leo . . . and then to the States to see all those Yankee cousins."

"But he was so happy here," Nance said. "We were happy."

"Jack's happy, Mum. Don't cry. I think you loved him more than I did, didn't you?"

Nance nodded. "Probably. If we hurry we could catch him at the station and talk him out of going."

Peanut shook his head.

Nance held him but knew he was holding her.

Spasms of temptation laced the boy's forehead. He couldn't cope with this barrel of instant feeling. But he learnt his first lesson in absolute acceptance. When you're swept you're swept. He wanted to hurt his mother. That was silly.

"I wish I could wave good-bye to Jack, but guess I'd only cry if I did. He'll be waving to us, but."

And when you're swept, Nance, no amount of looking back can recapture the emotion of a moment built on the wind blowing through your heart. When the moment is spent it's unchangeable.

Peanut felt unwalled and free when suddenly he realized

the fled emotion had not spirited him away in its blast. He touched his mother's shoulder.

"Mum? We'd better go. I'll be the last little boy there. And I don't want to be late on my first day." The chirp was gone.

Sadness made a wreath of Nance's lips. She stood up and gave him her hand and he led her downstairs. He waved through the shop window to his father and they walked up Cambridge Street, each measuring a new world with every step.

"Mum?"

"Yes?"

"There's a big feather missing from one of your hats. Don't look for it. I gave it to Jackie. He wanted a rebel cockade."

"Feathers are out," Nance said, sleep-wording. She squeezed his hand to let him know it was all right. Her other communicating centres were not functioning so well.

"And, Mum. Please tell the teacher my name is . . . Jim . . . not Peanut. Now don't forget, Mum."

Nance signalled agreement with another squeeze. He squeezed back. What a work of God a boy is! My son, James Oxford Delarue.

One day, in the magnitude of another time, she and Mitch Singleton were painting some deal-board furniture he had made when Grandad Singleton said, "Don't make a mess of your painting by trying to brush the flies off when it's wet, Mitchie. Let it dry properly overnight, then just flick them off in the morning. It's easy and not so sloppy. You can fix a lot of things that way, son."

"We're there, Mum," Jim said.

"Let me look at you for the last . . . or is it the first time? . . . Jim," Nance said. "Have you got your threepence? And a clean hanky?"

"We didn't forget anything, Mum. And you've given me three different clean hankies already, this morning."

Nance pouted, then smiled. "Yes, You've certainly got everything. And it's all before you."

"Gee!" Jim said, surveying the kids waiting outside Miss Bowen's office. "Have you ever seen so many clean little boys?"

"Never," Nance said. "And I warrant you never will either until the first day of school after the summer holidays."

Miss Bowen held no brief for sad-eyed parents who acted as if their offspring were being consigned to a fate worse than a dentist's chair.

"Good-bye, darling," Nance said hurriedly, then added melodramatically, "I'm going to the bank today to start an account for University like I said I'd do."

"Bye, Mum. Don't worry putting Jack's pyjamas back under the pillow when you're making the bed. He didn't take them because he'll be roughing it for a while."

Nance braced her eyes and walked away like a character out of *East Lynne*.

On the way home Mrs. Delarue stopped at the Death Seat. She hadn't sat there since the day Mitch Singleton went off to war. There she had opened his farewell gift — the alarm clock she cherished. A fragile thing made in Germany, ironically enough. It still played a centuries-old tune called "Lillibullero." An asterisk of memory.

Nance knew she would have married Mitch if he hadn't been killed in the Middle East. Perhaps, as Mrs. Singleton she wouldn't have been as sexually happy. On the other hand her powerful sexual instincts might never have been mined without Tony's assistance.

Remembering the night she and Mitch had had to leave a Kincomba newsreel theatre showing scenes of the London

Blitz made it easy for her to hear his hushed voice, see his nebula of tears. One horrible scene of a terrified child clutching a burnt armless doll had shattered him. That little girl hugging her doll with grim maternity but shedding no tears. Her dark baby eyes sentencing the world. How could people forget what Britain went through to win this world they had now.

"I can't take it, Nancy," Mitch said. "I have to go."

"What about University?"

"What has education got to do with existence?"

"I knew you'd go."

He was seventeen, a placid boy afraid of any temperamental flame. And the world was burning.

She was glad Peanut . . . Jim . . . was not like Mitch. Life was different. Not enough honourable people left in the world; honour meant being vulnerable — and sincerity had become rarer. Mitch had fought and died in a war but had never been a fighter. The world had lacerated those tender boys.

"Tony can be so bloody intransitive at times!"

She had to learn, too. The Mrs. Minivers were no longer Greer Garsons. And Jack Rivers was . . . Jack was a permutation of Mitch . . . gone. Connie was that part of Tony Mitch would have detested. But Connie was only a little girl. How could her eyes sometimes look as if she were prosecuting mankind. Mitch had been . . . maternal. Let's face that!

Nance decided not to make any more bargains with life. She had given up Mitch to war and accepted Tony in return; and what she hated most about it was that she had got the best of the haggle. All she now wanted was to retrieve the security Jack Rivers had given her.

If you go to the bank now, Nance, then go straight home, make the beds and put the vacuum cleaner once over lightly, you'll still have time to give Tony his coffee break. He does love that beer before lunch. Then you can do Connie her favourite toasted cheese sandwich for lunch.

"And don't burn the toast."

Fry some chips for Pea . . . Jim. Crisp! So that he can eat them out of a newspaper cornet. As long as you have Jim you'll have Jack. Oh well, come day, go day, God send Sunday.

"Come on, Jack, let's go . . . Oh, so what? I guess you'll be around one way or another, in and out of minds, for a while."

The town had wound itself up more automatically than Nance had. It began to drizzle. The wet gave a satin finish to the tarred streets, depriving them of their matt-working reality, robbing the cars of their antlike proficiency. Brakes screeched at other brakes. Life can be a bit of a drizzle at times.

The bank was open and quiet: when Mrs. Carstairs gave Nance a singular look Nance gazed right through her. Wait till they hang that on the line with their tattletale greys.

"I'll give it to you *straight*, Dell," Mrs. Allsop said. And she meant in the stadium of life. "That Nancy Delarue is a queer one."

The laundrette was a hive of women who, like drones, had rushed there with the first sparkle of rain as if the sun belonged to Haley.

Nance hummed past them, gave Tony a Mrs. Yankee Fixit grin and belted upstairs. She knew the sun would be back. "Jack Rivers said so, Mum." And Johnnie never lied. Technocrat and sometime-bore he might be, but Jack had the morality and internal strength of a chaste robot. She felt like a bee that had the bucket of a big flower all to herself . . . himself? And it was springtime.

"You done good, Nance!"

When she started making Peanut's bed and came across Jack's pyjamas, crushed but clean, among the linen limbo her intentions were to no avail. Tears assaulted her heart and she took the pyjamas back to her own bedroom and lay down with them, smelling them as though they were thornless roses. She began massaging her breasts. Soon she was masturbating — something she had not done since Antony had returned home from the war — finding it hard to concentrate on her fantasy and listen at the same time for Antony's (thundering) footsteps on the stairs. Jack possessed her.

"Oh, well, Nance, if this is incest, you can live with it." It was the greatest orgasm she had had since before Connie was born.

17

"IT'S THE WEDDING of this'ere year in spite of all the hoi polloi," Mrs. Allsop decreed. "And everybody will be at the kitchen tea because there's *no* reception."

"It's gonna be a humdinger," the kids said.

"It'll be bigger than the bloody sun in January."

That it turned out to be monstrous was no surprise. The only problem was where to put all the tendered food. Trifles, cakes, sandwiches, curried prawns, devil's fingers (a shishkabob of prunes strangled by bacon strips), Indian dicks (thin sausages), thick-dick saveloys (called starvers in the Depression), and much much grog. There was plenty of everything except married couples.

"I talked me missus inter goin' to Chadla to visit 'er sickie sister."

"For once I insisted that Cliff go to the Greyhounds at Kincomba. I wanted to be here free tonight. He can be such a wet blanket."

"If I don't get a screw tonight I'll unscrew my prick and donate it to the dog pound."

The night was Edenesque. A wedding-veiled marcasite moon, clouds as frail as moths, the perfume of spring camouflaging the sulphur. The frosted globes inside and outside the School of Arts glittered, making the old building crystalloid in the heart of Boomeroo. Several bullfrogs made unceasing noises like a paddle of young ducks.

It was a distillation of time. A night on which a man might predict there was no evil on earth . . . merely madness.

The women arrived dressed for launching. The men were strapped into their best suits. Unbreathing young girls in their first high heels looked breathlessly lovable.

"If I could take her cherry I'd whack off forever after, God."

Stalky young men, grazing like giraffes, hips as slim as snakes and horns as hard as tusks, squeezed closely past any skirt they could manoeuvre by. Kids in candy-court clothes yukked one another.

"You look wicked tonight," Darcy said to Goldie as they drove to their exuberant welcome.

"Not wicked enough to make me famous, unfortunately," she said.

"You look all woman."

"But I'm not all the women I want to be . . . yet."

"We'll have a great future."

"Let's live it as the day breaks. Today is fine. Tomorrow's predictably finer."

"And we love."

"I love you. Don't doubt that. Just never treat me like a second-class citizen. I'll be a good wife and lover . . . but no rib."

"OK," Darcy said. "You skip the apple and I'll ditch my fig leaf."

The young, the middle-aged and the old men trekked outside in twos and threes to pay homage to the first eighteen-gallon keg that Shake Downey and the Bulls had set up in the back garden on a discarded butcher's stump. The city visitors soon got the message of the way to the cold gold. When Duck Allsop's dirty big black retriever began to piss up the butcher's block it got about thirty thirsty feet in its gut.

The girls inside got together in giggles of geese while the orchestra, Mary Caddy and Her Merry Cadets, tuned up. Married women fussed over the food and arranged it in precise, almost religous order. Mrs. Allsop gave her ages of advice.

"Amy, *never* put Mrs. Cressy's lamingtons on the same plate as Mrs. Lawton's: if anybody criticizes or compliments that plate they both get ropable; and they're a pair of bloody old tartars when they get acidy ...

"Vera! Don't ever put two of old Mrs. Howe's trifles too close together. They're so full of rum if any of the ... genteeler ladies take seconds they'll get full as farts ...

"Look, Freda, we'll put all the lousy-looking sandwiches on that table near the back door where the men sneak in for a bite. Let them be sick ...

"*See this plate, Pearl* ... guard it with your life and don't give it to anybody at all except Father Barry when he drops in for a few fast sherries ... which he will ... and to sing ... which he certainly will."

There was no dearth of old dollies to make tea, pour sherry, scallop jelly with cream, titivate tablecloths, grade cupcakes and care for the few Shelley pieces — all sweet conniving veterans of the Sunday High Tea lamington litany, capable of carrying out in sinless silence the niceties that separated them from the females still intense enough to not-know their fates in these male-riffled waters.

"Heh ... did ya know Young Henry's found out about his wife and Ben Leslie? He's chatting her up about it now."

"They reckon Ben climbs up a woman like he was conquerin' Everest. Little battery-operated machines for ticklin' their clits . . . and pills to keep his rod like steel. They reckon!"

"Everyone in town knew before me," Young Henry was saying to his wife.

"That's how it is in this town," she said. "We should have gone to Sydney, to live like I wanted to."

"That's all you think of . . . Sydney, bloody, Sydney. Is it true?"

"True enough."

"I noticed you've been easily satisfied lately."

"*You've* been too easily satisfied lately," she said. "You should have done more than just notice."

"What's he got except money?"

"He leaves me feeling . . . beautiful inside myself, Henry." Her voice quivered; she felt as unstable as candle wax. "You're . . . like an engine. You leave me with the feeling my legs will never meet again."

"Sadie!" Young Henry was diverted by shock. "Well, are you coming home with me tonight?"

"You want me to?" Sadie's eyes were direct.

Young Henry adjusted his throat and pants — both torque-tight. He bulged more than ever where he was both famous and infamous. "That's not what I asked you."

"Where else could I go?" Sadie said. "To your mother's?"

Young Henry went back to the beer keg where the laughter was more paralytic than drunk. Randiness would resolve his and Sadie's problem.

There were a few simple speeches. Darcy's father had evidently been told to keep it brief, basic and unbantered. Uncle Old Mason spoke on behalf of Mrs. Killorn and Goldie. Ben Leslie welcomed the out-of-towners and even those who hated him were proud of him. Ben could lace words as well as he could unlace women. Goldie's boss made a corny speech about his loss being Darcy's all. He was the kind of man whose first words one remembered but whose last words were too long in coming.

When Mary Caddy and Her Merry Cadets went back to the old-time dance music it seemed time for the party to face factions. Some of the fat-dog and skinny-bat girls, resigned to indoor male shortages, danced together. Darcy mingled with the home owners and Goldie charmed the visitors. They bowled over a few barricades while the Cadets musicked away. The Merry Cadets were the teenage Tremayne triplets, Dixie, Dorothy and Dudley, whose names had been trampled into Dixie, Doxie and Duxie . . .

"You can fuck all three of 'em, but Duxie's the best screw."

"Their mother used to be Dolly Driver. She married Changa Tremayne. All those Drivers screwed."

Ah, the country life . . . the men weaving beer-bereaving memories, the women beginning to smoulder on Marsala.

Muriel O'Sullivan sang "Come Back Paddy Reilly."

Mrs. Allsop did not sing "A Gordon for Me," but "Last Farewell to Stirling," a song Goldie's Dad had loved. Mr. Killorn had been a greatly and townly loved horseman, who had suffered a fatal coronary while breaking in a young stallion. In the decision of the pubs, an envied way to go.

When it came to belting out a ballad, Mrs. Allsop was a professional: her voice could soar, loop lower than many, and hover higher than most. Before she finished her number even the keg came to a trickle:

> "Now fare you well for I am bound
> For twenty years to Van Diemen's Land;
> But speak of me and what I've done
> When I am far from Stirling . . . hoh!"

The locals tried to be polite even when they were at a loss. What can you say to city folk when you're telling them you have to jiggle the damper on a coal stove to wake up its dreaming embers first thing in the morning, and they look at you like as if you've been burying bombs under the Electricity Commission Building in Kincomba or Sydney or Newcastle?

Father Barry arrived almost as the signal for supper to begin.

" 'E arrives like Jesus for the Last Supper and eats like Judas."

The priest shook beneficient hands with the Church of England minister and kissed the Methodist minister's wife on the hand.

"She's French-Canadian, you know. They say she still secretly goes to confession."

"The good Father'll give her something big to confess if she ain't careful."

The wild Roman had a few sherries while demolishing his set-aside plate of goodies; sang "Boulavogue" in his fertile Irish baritone as though he had been racked by the English along with the martyr, Father Murphy; accepted his compliments like sponges dipped in Drambuie; and left like St. Peter before the third cock crowed.

Some said that the fancy Father's flamboyant version of "Boulavogue" was the real flame of the murphy that followed, although they had to admit Tony Delarue didn't help when he broke up the "Gypsy Tap" and insisted on singing "The Catalpa," without being sure of the words.

"That's my Dad singing," Jimmy Delarue said.

"Sounds more like my dog rootin' round with Alderton's chooks," Duck said; and Connie cuffed him.

Tony was in full sail:

"Come all you screw warders and jailers,
Remember Perth regatta day,
Take care of the rest of your Fenians,
Or the Yankees will steal them away.

Da-dum-da-dum-da-da!

You kept them in Western Australia
Till their hair began to turn grey,
When a Yank from the States of America
Came out here and stole them away.

The Georgette, *armed with bold warriors,*
Went out the poor Yanks to arrest,
But she hoisted her star-spangled banner,
Saying, 'You'll not board me, I guess.' "

He might have gone on till the next American election if Goldie's girlfriends had not hooted him in a dithery feminine way he loved rather than objected to.

"We are Ameri*cans* not Ameri*can'ts!*" Tony yelled as their slender horny fingers distracted him from the dias.

"More like Ameri*cunts*," someone said diligently.

The girls weren't as talented as they were ravishing and performed their agreed-upon chorus like gurgling virgins, forming a patulous pavilion of sex about Goldie:

"We're glad Darcy loves you;
Glad Darcy loves you . . .
You can't peel bananas,
You're no kind of cook . . .
But you'll make little Darcys
Without any book."

"Girls are getting risqué."

"It was always risky . . . even with a Frenchie."

Around the keg the men and foraging boys and collecting insects were initiating Darcy into a Boomeroo custom deadlier than fate and later than death, but better than never:

> *"Here's to Darcy, the stupid grub,*
> *Now he's gonna have to tub*
> *Every day and every night*
> *To keep his foreskin brighter'n white.*
> *So drink chuggalug, chuggalug, chuggalug."*

Things stayed on an even keel until Blowaway Sidey's widow appeared rather than arrived and rocked the boat by insisting upon drinking at the keg with the footballers. It was her voice not her presence that annoyed them; it was as shrill as her late hubby's referee whistle.

"Sends shivers down me and makes me feel like I'm offside!"

She was a xyster-voiced woman, whom other females detested and men ignored except for the time it took to seduce her . . . a shortening period. The footballers tossed to see who would cart her off and knock her off just to get rid of her.

Bible Jones sang "Land of Our Fathers" and they probably heard him in Wales. Some well-trained boys brought trays of shandies in for the ladies. A scrum of men went down to the back fence to leave the toilets free for the women. "See if you can piss on these fuckin' frogs and shut 'em up: we can't very well piss on the old dollies to shut *them* up."

None of the city friends or cousins was asked if he or she had a talent.

Miss Turn'er Downey sang "Once I Had Three

Brothers," unaware that one of them, Shake, had won the toss for Blowaway Sidey's widow, and that another, Brake, had caught Duxie Tremayne jacking off during a dance break and was presently rooting him under the building not more than six feet from her shoes.

"All those fuckin' Downeys can sing."

"An' all the singin' Downeys can fuck!"

Inside, sipping sherry while cleaning up the leftovers, literally and gastronomically, the gentle gender gossiped.

"A lot of this 'ere cookin' was done from bought packets."

"None of this Instant guck stands up."

"What's so new about that, Norma? My old man's been having instant ejaculation for twenty years. His certainly never stood up for long."

Mary Caddy had lost her Cadets, so Uncle Old Mason played his fiddle to give her a breather. Maureen Craig began to sing "The Boys from County Mayo" and a swarm of kids began a faltering barn dance which was soon a hive of misconstruction. Monte Howard offered to teach Connie Delarue to dance (she was uphappy in a dress). Duck Allsop started to teach his dirty big black retriever the barn dance in a hurry in case they made it Progressive.

Suddenly a loud voice from the back door reported in penetrating amazement: "One of them Sydney poofters just called Granfarver Jones a crazy bastard and pushed the lazy old cunt off his feet."

"Shoulda called him a lazy old cunt and pushed the crazy bastard off his feet."

" 'E's me mum's grandfather. Cop this."

"Why you lousy one-punch, king-hittin' bastard . . . you're hopeless without a fence paling."

The fighting spread like volcanic ash and people fell like human lava. Maureen sang on gallantly.

"Ouch! What's that for? I'm barman."

"I know, stupid! That's for leavin' the keg running, you great gink."

It was havoc until someone called out, "Hold it! They're doin' the Progressive Barn Dance. Everybody inside!"

They understood that command and downed fists like backward ballerinas attuned to applause rather than to perfection. The Progressive Barn Dance is the *only* dance all Australian men can do. It was criminal and a sign of gutlessness not to get up in it. They struggled in, puffed eyes lit, split lips sensuously shining in blood-lick, and picked up the first visible woman: whether she had a cup of tea or dishcloth or baby in her hands was immaterial. They joined the twin wheels of dancers to become part of the boisterous endlessness of this clumsy annular diffusion.

"Nice night, Mrs. Cressy. Your lamingtons were corken and ..."

". . . Hullo, Mrs. Howe. Still spry as ever. If I'm drunk it's 'cause I ate too much of your ..."

". . . You sang beaut tonight, Muriel. Better'n Maureen."

"Your hairdo musta cost a fortune, Mrs. Allsop. I can't see where it ends."

While the Progessive lasted, the magic, as unpolished as it was, existed. When it ended the aura petered out. Someone shouted, "Scots awa!" and the groups split as fast as multiplying virus.

There was a mad scramble to pack outside. The citysiders had become embroiled in the cult of the keg, and a host of them were wrestling the barrel. The Boomeroosters had enough enemies in their own ranks to continue the riot.

Mysteriously carried away by excitement, Mary Caddy bounced up and pounced into "The Gathering of the Clans." Maybe she merely thought a "Pride of Erin" danced at a Scots celebration might reconcile the forces.

Mrs. Allsop strutted along the trestles to the centre table and, with some hope in hades of overcoming the din, belted forth. The pitch and toss of the Donnybrook became the whirl and skirl of the braemar.

> *"The clans are gathering,*
> *Gather-ring, gather-ring!*
> *Through the deep glen*
> *And from faraway lands."*

"Wop! Take that, you bastard."
"Cop this, you lousy grub."
"How about this, you Cucumber cunt?"
Splop!
"Hey, Shake! It's me. Upsa! Your bruvver!"
"There's no brothers in drink and war."
Indoors Goldie exhibited her presents to a gobble of young ladies and courageous possible spinsters.

There were only two couples left dancing: the reconciled Young Henry Garsides, and old Mrs. Howe in floor-flogging lavender lace with Timmy Sweeny, who didn't want to get his face, body or dick injured because he had plans for the night.

> *"The clans are gathering,*
> *Gather-ring, gather-ring!"*

"Is this what you call a Real Catasterphe, Mum?" Jim Delarue said.

"I should think so," Nance said. "I can't imagine a more real catastrophe than your father in the morning."

"Hey, Peanut," Monte Howard said. "Come into the library an' I'll show you pictures of all the soldiers killed in the wars."

"All right," Jim said. "But I'm Jim now, and I'm not thinking of dying these days. My drongo mate at school,

Justin Cameron, said there's no ice cream when you're dead."

"All those men died for their country," Monte said, indicating the framed heroes. "And they all came from Boomeroo."

"Jack Rivers would die for his country if he had one," Jim said.

"Oh?"

"I had a letter from him. Grandma Leo posted it for him. He's in the Islands. On his way to Korea to make sure everything gets cleaned up properly." His keen eye picked out Mitchell Singleton's photo. "My Mum's got him in our family album. He's that boy of barely-nineteen-summers my mother talks a lot about."

"You want to hear a poem that reminds me of Jack Rivers?" Monte said: after all, Mitch Singleton was his uncle.

"Yes."

> " 'Somewhere or other he's knocking about.'
> Knocking about on the runs of the West,
> Holding his own with the worst and the best,
> Breaking in horses and risking his neck,
> Droving or shearing and making a cheque;
> Straight as a sapling — six-foot, and sound,
> Jack is all right when he's knocking around."

"That's My Jack all right."

The clans were still gathering in the drubbed garden: some shaping up like Dave Sands and some like bags of shit.

Ben Leslie consoled Mrs. Killorn.

"But Goldie wouldn't want it any other way," Gladys said. "Why aren't *you* out there, Ben? I'm sure Darcy is."

"Because the older I get the more I think about myself and the less I care about more people," Ben said.

"That's always been you, Ben."

"I have this talent for learning late in life."

"Bosh!" Goldie's mother said, determined to be neither brow- nor brain-beaten. "Men like you never learn."

Goldie interrupted. She sparred around Ben, shuffling her feet like Errol Flynn in *Gentleman Jim*. "Come-ona fight!"

"Now, Goldie," Ben said reprovingly. "I was telling your mother how I've changed in middle age."

Mrs. Killorn left them to their nothing.

"You've been over forty since you were twenty-one, Ben."

"I mean in my heart."

"Keep your reconstituted heart," Goldie said, swinging him in a reel and singing softly: "The Leslies and Darcys, the Bens and the Halls . . . The Killorns and the Joneses . . . The Allsops and all . . ."

"I mean I don't bleed anymore when someone cries," Ben said as she dipped under his arm.

"Maybe you cry when someone else bleeds," she said. "I hope so."

The clans were still fighting so determinedly the outdoor shithouse was on the verge of collapsing in the centre of battle.

"You'll need me," Ben said.

Goldie stopped in his track. "As I have to be a woman, I'm determined not to be half a woman; so I'm settling for a whole man instead of half a man."

"You are a bitch!"

"But not on heat. Thank you for everything, Mr. Leslie. Especially for the Coalport dinner set. Every time I eat from it I'll digest a little of you. Does that make your latent heart happy?"

"Good-bye, Mrs. Hall . . . I'll send you Mrs. Beeton's cookbook some time."

"The Campbells and Camer-rons . . .
Grants and MacDonalds . . .
The bonnie wee Gordons
And men of Monroe . . ."

"Ain't you the poofter that picked on Granfarver Jones
in the first place . . . you chicken coot!"

"Yeah, but I'm too buggered to fight anymore."

"Tha's OK. Why'n't you kill the old crap bag while you
'as at it?"

". . . to join in the reel
With the lads of McNeil,
While you swirl to the skirl
Of the pipes of McRae."

A drinking man's energy is apt to flag before his spirit,
so most of the adversaries finally (and suddenly) sagged
into one another's arms and staggered back to the next keg.

The kids were now slipping round the vacant dance
floor on their backsides in the fine candle wax. Young
Henry and his young missus skedaddled home like a horny
pair of rhinos: her body could already feel the irruption of
his colossal prick and her throat the surgery of his cuneal
tongue.

Timmy Sweeny walked old Mrs. Howe home.

"I like old ladies," Timmy said.

"That's nice," the old dolly burbled.

"I mean I *love* 'em . . . you know."

"But I'm eighty," she said, fuller than any of her spiked
trifles had been.

"Mum says you're close to ninety," Timmy said. "But I
don't care. I love that flabby old flesh old ladies have on
their arms . . . and legs."

"Oh, my God," Mrs. Howe said, and flaked out conveniently just as they reached her canvas-covered front veranda.

Timmy lifted her tenderly onto the sun lounge, undressed her painstakingly, then made good flabby use of her body. He revived her later and whispered into the lardy old ear, "Gobble me off . . . I wanna come again."

The old dear did not know what he meant, but smiled wistfully, so he used her again much to her conscious delight, until she murmured, "You can come here any time you want to, Timmy-boy Sweeny."

Those Bulls who still imagined they were up to stud standard whisked . . . dragged Darcy off to a Chadla brothel and brought him back suffering from an inguinal strain just as the moon was vanishing. They stripped him, roped him, and left him on the Death Seat.

When Constable Hervey did his special delivery beat early that morning, the groom was gone. "A bloody Houdini," the policeman said to the dew-pearling wood.

Goldie had cheated and bribed Duck Allsop to help her cut through the heavy ropes and deliver her groom from his malaise tower. But she did not pay Duck to keep his mouth shut.

So the Allsop brat added Darcy's to his store of genitalia dimensions. "He's got no foreskin at all and it ain't as big as Young Henry's."

"Whose is?"

"But he's got the biggest dangliest balls I ever saw. When Goldie kissed him and called him Arsy Darcy he got a horn and it was real straight. No bend in it. I fought they all had a bend in 'em . . . what you get from jackin' off. Oh . . . an' he's real hairy, too . . . bloody hairier than the barber's floor. Nearly as hairy as Bonnie Prince Charlie."

"Who?"

"My dirty big black retriever!"
"That thing's got a name?"
Thought you'd never ask.

Of all the valley towns guarded by that untouched battlement, Mount Kaiser, and protected by the half-sheared parapets of the Terribana and Booradeela hills, Boomeroo — close to their high hinge — was the most sheltered from man's intentions and God's mistakes.

To feel safe you only had to look at the tremendous flanks of eucalyptus trees crowding most of the footpaths and back yards of the town, camouflaging what for the most part was a shishkabob of houses on narrow serried streets, and remember: those people in those houses were you.

Ah, Boomeroo . . . some day I'll find you.

Wait for me! Wait for me!

"Don't go! Don't go!"

18

"So JACK RIVERS made it to the Islands." Tony was really more absorbed in tenderizing his temples.

"At least from Boomeroo to Boroko." Nance looked like the cat who caught the canary and was still playing with it. "That boy's life has just begun."

"I'm getting up real early in the morning to go mush-rooming," Connie announced loud enough for Jim to hear her above the piano noises he was making. "And I'm taking Jim with me. He's old enough to get out of this damn crib."

Jim stopped playing: he had decided to learn since Connie unceremoniously kicked the piano, called it a three-legged bugger, and pronounced her musical career kaput from that moment. Jim was intent enough, and Connie was already referring to him as Brat Mozart.

"I've always wanted to go mushrooming real early one morning." Her brother snapped the piano closed.

"That'll be nice," Nance predicted.

"Of course, you'll have to wake me," Connie warned him.

"I will, I will, I will," Jim said.

"How's school going?" Tony was sipping coffee as if it cost a hundred bucks a tongueful.

"All right," Jim said. "But I got a pretty scottie teacher, Dad."

"You're lucky."

"He means his teacher is a grumpy old bat," Connie informed their father.

Tony's eyes painfully half-circled his hung over world, but he grinned prayerfully and raised his eyebrows acknowledgingly.

Jim put his practice piece in the piano stool, sighed thoughtfully, and said, "Wish I had a few more fingers, but."

"Bet your mate, Jack Rivers, could do a five-finger exercise with three," Connie said.

The quiet was elaborate.

"Connie," Tony said softly, "if we do talk about Jack, or if we must, we'll do it with respect or not at all. Understand?"

"Yeah."

"Yeah what?"

"Yes, Dad, I understand." But rebellion, not compromise, was Connie's true nature. She added, "That's a switch, coming from you. You never did like him because he was black." She was walking past her father at the time on her way upstairs, where she spent a lot of time alone these days.

Tony grabbed her wrist and jerked her to him. "*What* did you say, my girl?"

"Mum!" Connie said. "He's hurting me."

"Oh, Tony," Nance muttered, "let her go and let it be."

"No!" Tony was adamant, and twisted his daughter's wrist a little more. "I want her to repeat what she said in case I was hearing things."

"I said," Connie said, "you never liked Jack Rivers because he was an Abo."

He let her go in dumb surprise, and she went stubbornly on upstairs as she had intended. Tony was looking at Nance in aggrieved amazement.

"Nance, believe me, I swear to God I never knew that kid was a nigger."

His wife looked back at him perilously close to tears and said, "I don't believe you." She went out to the kitchen.

Tony bolted after her. "Well, how the hell did you know?"

"I was able to assume, the same as Connie, that he was." Nance shook his hand off. "I guess you just never listened."

His belligerence gone, Tony put his coffee cup in the sink and left without another word. He sank into his armchair as resigned as if he were the *Titanic*.

Jim walked quietly and resolutely across to his father, stood within the inlet of his Dad's strong legs, and said, "I believe you, Daddy." He then inched closer and leant over until their crotches kissed and planted his lips to Tony's forehead.

His father came alive. "Hey!" He stood his son back and scrutinized him, and made an all-Australian effort. "How about comin' to the footie with me?"

"I'd like that even better than mushroomin'," Jim said. "But I better go up and see Connie now."

"Right!" Tony was Tony. "That's a great idea. You go up and see how Connie is." He grinned. Mr. Yankee Fixit, alive and well and striving. "And I'll go out and wipe up for Mum. Give 'er a shock." The conspirators smiled at each other.

When Jim rode into the bedroom Connie was lying fast asleep on top of her bed with her clothes on, so he got off his horse and tiptoed past her to the window, wishing he had the guts to wake her. He knew he shouldn't be alone. Looking out, across to the school yard, it overcame him again and he began to whispersing:

> *"Lavender's blue, dilly-dilly,*
> *Lavender's green . . .*
> *When I am King, dilly-dilly,*
> *You'll be my Queen."*

The tears glazed his cheeks as he sang. He licked the first one to reach his mouth, and said aloud, "You're *My Jack*. You'll always be My Jack wherever you are."

His sobbing woke Connie. She got up somberly, but by the time she was at his side her heart was full of his trouble. She put an arm around his shaking small shoulders and said, "I'll make it up to you, little brother. I promise. Even if it takes me all my life. I do promise!"

When Tony and Jim went off to that first particular football game, Nance and Connie viewed each other grudgingly from new angles. They knew they would be left to face a fairly comfortable feminine future in a land where, and in a time when, even women with undeniably beautiful faces and loaded with brains could still have questionable futures, especially in the country, where to be married was to be marred.

"Oh, for Godsake, Bill, do you think I was so incomplete I *had* to marry you?"

"Watch it, Kevin! You're driving me close to going back to being the intelligent woman I was before I married you."

"Of course I never helped you in the fuckin' business! Do you think having five kids and doing for them every inch of every hour of every mile was sitting on my arse eating chocolate?"

"Good-bye, you bastard. You've just got one mate too many."

For these women, the transition was too ramifying to be

of ány help at that stage. Too promising too suddenly. Half these women, born early in the century, were too enmeshed in Victorianism to escape; the other half were too instantly rebellious to have planned their freedom. And too many of them were too bitter even to hope for their daughters.

On that Saturday afternoon most of the men went to the Rugby Union field to watch the Chadla Chickens make mullock of the still-pissed Boomeroo Bulls.

"Not to worry! It's for a good cause."

It was a Dave Sands Benefit Game: Sands had recently been killed in a road accident at Dungog. He was a fighter; he was young, and his future was illuminated. The greatest local-bred goer since Les Darcy: he was more than just a champ. Dave Sands won 93 out of 104 bouts . . . 60 knockouts. This outstanding person was a Middleweight Champion, a Light-Heavyweight Champion, a Heavy-weight Champion, Australasian and Empire Champion. A fighter whom Sugar Ray Robinson, Jake La Motta and even Rocky Graziano had avoided, and whom Randy Turpin and Bob Olsen were sorry they met. He was an Aboriginal. He was the boy from Burnt Ridge. And Tony (the torn American) was able to tell his son, Jim, all this at the benefit game. It was pub lore, and Tony had done his homework well.

Meanwhile (back in Victoriana) a formidable huddle of the football fans' women waited outside the Church of England church, before and after the wedding of the valley year.

"That gang of dames that hang round the churches on Saturday arvos to watch the weddin's . . . they all frustrated or somethin'?"

"Shit no, they mainly go just to see who's preggie before they get married."

"There'd be some bloody good forwards among that mob of sheilas if we could get 'em to play Rugby. An' Boomeroo really needs a first-rate hooker."

"Like Feet-Feet Anderson or that young Big Myrtle Worthington."

Goldie wore a wanton volume of white parramatta under a dress of sensational sendal that was close to colourless, scalloped at the hem, puffed at the elbows and welded to the waist. More Royal Doulton than Dresden. She looked like Elizabeth Bennet, but her waiting Wuthering Darcy was more Brontë than Austen. She carried guelder roses, which Blowaway Sidey's widow later frantically fought for and caught.

" 'Taint fair . . . she was offside again!"

Those early enough to pack themselves into the weatherboard church heard the lovers vow to each other in sincere, hoarse whispers.

"Amelia Emily Killorn?"

"I do."

"Darcy Adlington Hall?"

"I do!"

"Adlington? Don't tell me he's a throwback . . . to Addle'eaded 'Arry Adlington?"

Wait till they hang that one on the butcher's hook on Monday morning.

"He was a Catholic, you know . . . but didn't turn."

"Into what, Millie? A pillar of bloody salt? My Reggie wasn't . . . but he didn't turn either." Mrs. Allsop rose magniloquently for all religions when she added, "He just never looked back!"

While the knotted lovers were in the presbytery signing pledges to God and society, Jerry Kyle sang, his untouched soprano imbuing Sjoberg's words with a clarity matching the sunny afternoon.

Before the newlyweds drove off, their car went round the block and came back past the church where Darcy had been instructed to throw two handfuls of threepences to the kids waiting with their mothers.

"Why?"

"Because I want you to. When I was a little girl they used to throw pennies to the kids. Not many; but you'd never believe the things I managed to buy with that wedding money. I had big grabby hands and was tall for my age.

"You haven't changed a bit," Darcy said.

"Don't laugh, Adlington. These kids will remember today; that's why I made it threepences."

"I love you, Amelia Emily. Already you're more of a woman and less of a female."

"I did it with what you gave me," Goldie said capriciously. "But beware! Now I intend to become more of a *person*."

"I never expected you to be a whole glory of women," Darcy said. "Don't blame me for the shifts in the attitudes of men. Get stuck into Helena Rubenstein . . . swab that cosmetic mob who bribe women to be frail to delude men."

"Your Boomerese is already showing," Goldie said.

As they motored into their refrangible enchantment it seemed Jerry Kyle's pure voice still hovered in the Saturday sunlight. In the spring, Down Under, the Pacific air has a strange lingering quality, like some incessant wave in search of the perfect beach, and those soprano tears, weeping from the webbed silhouette of the willows on the outskirts of town, assailed their promises:

> *Loved one, I bless every hour we share,*
> *Deep . . . deep in our rapture,*

In silence and prayer.
You show me life's glory;
The earth and the heavens are mine;
Time seems everlasting . . . and love . . .
Love is divine.

Men and women ask from each other things that gods could not cling to for a lifetime.

As they walked home from the church, Nance and Connie indulged in a long slice of silence. Connie was clutching a load of threepences she intended to die with.

"I do love you, you know, Connie," Nance said jumpily.

"I know, Mum," Connie said, as if she had stuffed her voice up her jumper. "Just because I haven't got a dimple doesn't mean I'm dumb. If you promise not to bawl I'll tell you something. I love you a lot."

"Oh . . . Con-neeee . . ."

"Oh, God . . . here come the tears! I knew I shouldn't have told you that. Can't you, at least, wait till you get home, Woman?"

"I'll try." Nance sniffed, wielding a handkerchief.

After the footie, Tony took Jim to the pub with him and told him to play with the grubstake of kids on the fringe of the makeshift beer garden. "I'll only have a few," Tony said. "Then we'll buy some fish and chips to take home for supper . . . *tea!*"

"Take your time, Dad," Jim said. "There's sure to be some drongos I know from school that I can play with."

"We're mates?" Tony said.

"Bet ya bottom dollar," Jim said.

"God," Tony said, confounded. "God . . . and to think I nearly lost you."

This, then, was where our young unsung hero and

heroine, James Oxford Delarue and Constance Radley Delarue, grew up in yesterday's harmony, in a town where the Death Seat, a shattered old tree beaten into a pew, had taken on a cathedral of meanings. These were the people they knew in the hills that surrounded them. This was the life they loved and the life they lived, to which they generally surrendered. Here was where they would prefer to die. Their home, their heaven, their hell and their Xanadu. But these years are gone and the values involved vanished. Ravished.

Yet, wherever this place may now be, as long as it exists somewhere, Jack Rivers is safe. In this world . . . where the world once belonged.

19

MANY MANY years afterwards — long after James Delarue had flown the coop — when Connie Delarue was married and leaving home she finally opened her copper-heavy stool money box. Flattened deep under a Fort Knox of pennies and halfpennies, threepences and sixpences, garnished by a few one- and two- and five-cent pieces, was Jack Rivers's rebel cockade, stolen from Nance's hat and hidden in the safest place in the world.

And long long years after that, when Nance Delarue died — long after Tony had made his pilgrimage to Ohio and died of a stroke there — while her eldest grandson, John Mitchell Delarue, was packing her clothes in boxes to send to the Smith family, he found, at the back of her best lingerie drawer, a pair of little boy's winter pyjamas: the ironed-on name tag said they belonged to Jack Rivers.

As he folded them to put aside to take home to his own little boy, Antony Rivers Delarue, a small savings bank book fell from the pocket. It had been opened in September, 1952, with a ten-shilling deposit, by Nancy Delarue

(as trustee for) Jack Rivers. For almost five years, somebody had banked ten shillings each month. The final
balance — including interest — on the last line of the last
page showed thirty-four pounds, three shillings and eight
pence.

"I wonder how the hell he came by that name," John
Mitchell muttered.

Nobody ever knew, but it lived on.

Who said that death is oblivion?"

"I fuckin' don't know; but I reckon a man's strength
must sorta depend on his fantasies."

Somewhere in the years between, someone painted on
the underpass graffiti wall this legend:

JACK RIVERS WAS A CHICKENPRICK . . .

HE SHOULDA STOOD HERE

Saw My Jack today . . .
And as he turned away
I saw a tear within his eye
And wondered why . . .
I wondered why
They sent my Jack away.
Seems only yesterday . . .
But he'll come back to me
And we will be . . .
Yeah, we will be!

RADsong

Paul John Radley was born in Newcastle, Australia, in 1962 and attended high school through grade ten. *Jack Rivers and Me*, completed a year later, was the first recipient of the Australian/Vogel Literary Award for fiction and was published in Australia in 1981. His second novel, *My Blue-Checker Corker and Me*, appeared there in 1982; his third, *Good Mates!*, which completes the Boomeroo Trilogy, is forthcoming. Paul Radley rooms at the Crown and Anchor Hotel in Newcastle, where he is at work on his fourth novel. He also works part time as a bartender, plays Rugby Union, and "rages" at discos. Of his family Paul Radley says, "I belong to a large family within a labyrinthine family of endless talkers, from the articulate outgoing to the going-nowhere ocker, and there is nothing I haven't heard about living together, loving, being, and hating together, or apart. *And* I'm the only person in this world who ever slept with Jack Rivers . . . well, maybe except Nance."